T0068151

# CONFLICT

# CONFLICT

*In My City of Brotherly Love*

Roger Colley

# CONFLICT
# IN MY CITY OF BROTHERLY LOVE

iUniverse books may be ordered through booksellers or by contacting:

iUniverse
1663 Liberty Drive
Bloomington, IN 47403
www.iuniverse.com
844-349-9409

ISBN: 978-1-6632-5945-5 (sc)
ISBN: 978-1-6632-5946-2 (e)

Library of Congress Control Number: 2023924601

Print information available on the last page.

iUniverse rev. date:  12/29/2023

# Setting The Stage

This is the story of Joe Robinson. And it's also a story about human behavior and achievement. We begin with Joe as a 14 year old boy about to enter high school. He is black. He lives in a modest row house in a rough neighborhood in North Philadelphia, an area above the sparkling historic City Hall in central Philadelphia and near the heavily attended, sprawling urban campus of Temple University on Broad Street.

As the hot humid summer winds down, Joe will end his long days at a nearby playground with its two basketball courts and begin attendance at the nearby public high school. The Philadelphia Public School District has over 200,000 kids attending some 200 schools. The brighter, or luckier, kids attend the dozens of catholic or charter schools where discipline is stronger and the learning environment richer. A few even make the next step up and attend private schools or even get scholarships to suburban private schools. But not Joe.

The Robinson family is not typical in America, but not all that unique in its neighborhood. Philadelphia is known for its beautiful suburbs with their lovely homes, first class private schools, fancy private country clubs and its downtown with its Independence Hall, Constitution Center and its Museum of the American Revolution, the birthplace of our free nation.

But its industrial center, the heart 120 years ago of our United States industrial and commercial nation, once the home of Stetson hats and Baldwin locomotives, has now given way to many unkept, unsafe neighborhoods with a failing public school system despite the valiant efforts of so many well-meaning individuals and institutions.

Marvin Robinson served in the Vietnam conflict, fortunately unharmed. Upon discharge he married his sweetheart Sarah and landed a job with a home renovation company in North Philadelphia. His parents had come to Philadelphia from Georgia for employment during the first World War. Marvin was their only child as Marvin's mother had developed childbirth complications. Marvin's father had severe heart disease which Marvin unfortunately inherited. Marvin's dad died at age 52. Marvin later died of abrupt cardiac arrest at age 54.

While Marvin was serving in the Army, girlfriend Sarah, a very bright teenager, was able to graduate high school with high honors and then attend the first historically black college in the United States, Cheyney University in the Philadelphia suburbs. Back home after the war, Marvin kept talking about "discipline, discipline" and all its benefits, and Sarah would reply repeatedly with a frown "yes, yes, my man, I have discipline too with all the learning I'm going through, and at least I did learn to speak proper English". Sarah landed a rewarding job as a legal assistant with a prestigious downtown law firm. But she never landed the funding to apply to law school.

Marvin and Sarah had three healthy children, two bright boys who upon adulthood moved to the West Coast for better job opportunities and one daughter, Beatrice, who never married but had a daughter she named Ella. Beatrice was never sure which of the guys she played around with was Ella's father. No one volunteered. Despite the discipline lessons of her parents, Beatrice grew up in the new age of the so called 'sexual revolution' with free sex and foul language becoming so common on TV, in magazines, and in the movies. Her brothers, James and Michael, were sharp and disciplined, had excelled in school, but Beatrice just plain missed out. Not knowing who Ella's father was, Ella kept her last name Robinson. Then Ella fell into the same immorality trap as her mother Beatrice. Along with free sex, a new drug culture was rapidly expanding. At age 18 she became pregnant by who knows who, and she went on to have three children, William, Etta and Joe. No fathers present – a true Philadelphia problem. All still Robinson's.

So now we have it. The stage is set. The year 2023. Brother William Robinson age 18, part of an established drug dealing ring, making enough money that he rented the house next door to locate his 60-year-old grandmother, MomMom Beatrice, and his 85 year old great grandmother, wise old Mama Sarah. Sister Etta age 16, falling right in line, pregnant and trying to figure if the future dad will fess up. And brother Joe age 14 with a loving 35 year old Mom Ella, who is holding down a commercial cleaning job and rarely home.

Mama Sarah

I

MomMom Beatrice

I

Mom Ella

I

William, Etta, Joe

# PART ONE

PART ONE

About three weeks before facing up to feeling bold enough to walk into that big high school, one of the older kids at the playground who Joe had become friendly with gave him a cut out magazine article to read. The bigger kid had been friendly with Joe all summer as Joe seemed to exude lots of speed and hustle on the court even though the bigger kid demanded the ball all the time and took all the shots. The pick-up games were rough. Punching, cursing, and fouling were common. Joe admired this older kid because he seemed so much stronger and tougher than the others. Joe took the folded up two pages home and read them slowly and carefully three times before his mom called the home phone and said whichever kids were home to go next door to Mama Sarah's house for dinner as she had to work late that evening. Joe didn't always believe these stories, but whatever, Joe loved his great grandmother more than anyone and anything else in the world. She without hesitation was always so kind and so wise, never failing to give Joe all that he would want to eat plus the treats, and she also extended her words of wisdom, words that William and Etta sometimes seemed to miss in their understanding. But Joe was never too young to dismiss her constant advice. He was open to learning.

The magazine article was written by a sportswriter trying to make the point about how black athletes have progressed so far that they now dominant the pro football and basketball leagues. He was asking why? The writer emphasized the point that part of the reason is their natural strengths, perhaps genetically going back to their roots as strong field hand slaves or perhaps their dedication to developing strong bodies to overcome the difficulty in dominating in the mental world due to historic racism. This was difficult journalism for young Joe to comprehend, but the only reason for him to read it three times was the part about describing a young black kid in the South who, in desiring to play football some 60 years ago, decided to compete on physical strength. But he had no gym to go to. So, at home, he started to do sit-ups and pushups over and over again, eventually a super number per day. The boy got into a major university in the South, became first team All-American, voted the best college player in the nation, and played many years in the pros.

Joe was not a reader, in fact not dedicated to anything scholarly or any particular subject except playground basketball. But the story of that young kid in the magazine article about making something of himself really caught Joe's attention. Maybe if I start doing that, he thought, maybe I can be a better basketball player with those bigger, rougher kids. Maybe I can be in better position to face those wild high school kids too in a few weeks. All I hear about is the bullying, the fighting that goes on around that school, and William, my drop out brother, will not be there to protect me. That did it. Tonight, before bed I'll start, I'll hit the floor, he vowed to himself. His mind and chest seemed to burst with excited enthusiasm. It was a good feeling, but first to Mama Sarah's house for dinner.

The front porch of the house next door, occupied by Mama and Grandmom thanks to the generosity of big brother William, was glaringly much cleaner, neater, and more nicely plant decorated along with several comfortable looking chairs than Joe's porch front occupied by Mom, William and Etta. Joe knew that was all due to Mama Sarah's work ethic, even at 85 years old, but that reality was not one Joe gave a second thought to. In fact, Mama Sarah's house front looked like a strange stand out compared to all the other row homes on the block, what one might describe as a typical picture of one of Philadelphia's scenes of "poverty". Sarah knew fully well her home city had thousands of beautiful homes in many historic sections of the city, even many fancy row homes, but no way was she going to let her home be dragged down by the ongoing deterioration of her neighborhood.

In this section of town, front doors were always kept locked, so Joe calmly knocked and waited, as he had forgotten his key. It was sister Etta who opened the door for him as she also got the message that Mom would be home late. Etta returned to the small dining room while the kitchen flavors lured Joe right into the kitchen where Mama Sarah looked busy doing whatever over the stove. As usual, she turned and smiled at him and softly said in her usual friendly tone.

"Indeed, indeed, it is such a pleasure to have you, young man. How goes it, today?"

"Played b-ball again, Mama, all afternoon. It was hot. I'm thirsty, I'm starved."

"Okay, okay, look in the refrigerator, sweetheart. There's some Coke in there. You know where the glasses are…. And after dinner I want to have a little chat with you."

Oh no, thought Joe, as he followed her directions for a welcoming cold drink. The usual stuff, but I know I'll be listening to her. Oh well, usually I do hear her out. She means good. But soon I gotta get home to my room to start my new workout. But I will remember to say, as she has told me a thousand times, "thank you for dinner ma'am, nice of you to have me." 'Manners', she calls them.

As usual, the dinner was delicious. Very little talk, to Joe just some unintelligible chatter between Grandma "MomMom" Beatrice and Mama Sarah. Mother and daughter, while granddaughter Etta as usual very quiet. Upon learning she was pregnant a couple of months ago, she seemed very sullen. She use to laugh a lot with Joe and carry on with silly games, but no more. Joe didn't try to reason why the change in disposition.

After dinner, the dishes were quickly cleared by the three females. Beatrice and Etta remained in the kitchen to clean up. Sarah pointed her finger at Joe and directed him to the living room. This procedure had occurred so many times before. A great grandmother giving her beloved great grandson a lecture on being a "good boy," more specifically "stay away from the gangs, don't get into drugs like your brother William, respect the girls in your school, be obedient to your teachers, don't play with your friends' guns, listen to your Mom when she tells you something, don't skip school, pay attention in your classes, learn something." But tonight was a little different.

"Sit down next to me here young man," she began. "You know, I'm always telling you how to behave. I know," she sighed softly, "it probably goes in one ear and out the other, but I do know son I do really love you, and I think you also love me, and respect me. You have never sassed me or argued back, so maybe someday my messages to you will really sink in. I pray so." Her tone of voice continued on gently, not demanding, easy for Joe to listen to. He truly did love this woman, so much more than any other person in his life.

"So Joe, do you hear them in the kitchen? Listen. They are arguing. Grandmother and granddaughter. What I'm going to tell you is that this is natural, it's common, it's universal, it's everywhere, it's a basic, normal part of our human nature.

It's called 'conflict'. No two people agree on everything. You have it on the basketball court?"

"Yea, sure, all the time Mama. We argue, we fight. What are we arguing about? I don't even know."

"Classic, my boy. You're 14. You're developing. You understand male/female, making babies. Big debate in this whole country. Does the female have the right over her own body to decide if she wants to deliver that new whatever – baby, child, fetus, person … or to abort it, get rid of it … or does that new person developing in there, in her womb, have the right to live, a person protected by the United States Constitution, and if you abort it you have killed it … or is there some in between solution. Joe, should we people decide this, or the politicians, or some rights groups on either side? So your grandmom in there is arguing for Etta to have an abortion, get rid of this baby, you are only 16 she says, so don't repeat some of our mistakes. You can probably have it done for free…. But your sister says she wants more time to decide. She hears it's heartwarming to care for a baby and see it grow, and that there are all kinds of benefits to help out, welfare and all. So the two of them in there cannot agree. They are in conflict."

Joe looked at his Mama bewildered. "Why you tellin' me this? I got nothin' to do with it."

"Sweetheart, I'm telling you this because we are your family, but you are about to see a lot more conflict beyond your grandmom and sister and your fighting on the basketball court when you enter that high school in a few weeks. Guns, knives, girls, bullies, student/teacher harassments, anger, fights – I want you prepared."

"Come on Mama. What are you talkin' bout? I gotta get home." Feeling a little bit annoyed at all this deep stuff, but trying hard not to show it, what was on Joe's mind at this point was getting to those situps and pushups. Joe's mind could not seem to focus on what his great grandmother was trying to get across to him – conflict, abortion.

"Sure, I understand my dear boy. This is really deep stuff. I'm reading your mind. But I'll explain more about all this. I just want to teach you that their argument in there is friendly, but sometimes violence seems the only solution to our differences, but sometimes, many times, we can resolve these conflicts without resorting to violence."

Joe couldn't wait to get home to his bedroom. Start with ten of each, then add five more a day. Then spread out the routine morning, afternoon and night.

# 2

It turned out that Ella was working almost everyday to well past dinner time, so Joe and Etta were going to dinner at Mama's house almost every evening for dinner that August. At least her air conditioners were working fine during these hot summer days and evenings along with the good fortune that Grandmom Beatrice was doing a fine job shopping almost daily for the finest dinner foods she could buy during her daily trips out. William was providing her with a weekly stipend from his earnings, and along with generous food stamps the family qualified for, there was no absence of good meals at Mama's home. Joe did feel a little upset though that his big brother rarely came to dinner. Joe would have to stay up late at night just to say "hey" to him as he came into their shared bedroom and settled into the twin bed next to his. Many evenings William did not appear at all. It was beyond Joe's comprehension as to what all brother William was doing with his time. Something 'bout a drug gang', he thought. Puzzling, but Joe's mind did not dwell on it.

For Joe, the slight downside to having dinner at Mama's was that she always pulled him into her living room after dinner to go on with her "chats", as she called them, even though she did 90% of the chatting. She was unaware that he had his new workout constantly in mind. Inside his mind and body, he now felt compelled. Actually, it was a good sensation.

This particular evening, Mama Sarah started on a very different subject, one that Joe could easily understand but one Joe thought had no relevance to him. He was a "good" boy, never getting disciplined for bad behavior in grade school or junior high school, never hurting anyone at the playground, never stealing anything. He never thought twice about it. It was well maybe just natural, compared to so many other kids he knew. He was totally unconscious of his great-grandmother's continual influence over his young years, conveying a sense of good behavior, an invisible sense of discipline.

"Joe," Mama Sarah began after a wonderful dinner that left Joe full and content. "I have to say I am very happy with you, about you. Your behavior has been really good. I know all about it. I just had to tell you that."

Sitting side by side on the comfortable living room couch, Joe turned and looked quizzically at his great grandmom. What is she talking about, he wondered. She was smiling.

"Joe," she repeated. "You don't have to say anything. Just listen. I'm not going to let this go in one of your ears and out the other. I'm going to make my point. Listen, I did go to college many years ago. I did study psychology and human behavior. I understand that each of our brains are slightly different, but that we do end up with some common behaviors. Most of us

9

act in a way that gives us the best advantage, sometimes that means cooperating with, helping each other, helping those in need, like you might help MomMom set the table because you are hungry, but sometimes we act aggressively, possibly even violently, if that is what we feel is to our advantage. Someone breaks in through our front door to steal something and you might run away and hide, or you might start throwing punches at the guy. So, who knows how **your** brain works Joe, but it is your brain making you act the way you do. Our first reactions to what's going on start with our emotions not our reasoning. So far, it has been natural for you not to look for or cause trouble. But Joe, I want you to understand that the reason why we have so many religious practices, school rules, government laws, is because so many of us can at times be disorderly, and we need orderly behavior for all of us to move on without violence. So, my boy what I want you to understand is that as you move on to this high school soon, you are going to see kids on both sides, some orderly and some disorderly. I'm telling you that your future life, your successes ahead, can continue on the orderly side, the good behavior side, and then you will find happiness in your future life, not chaos and despair." She finally paused.

Joe looked right at her now. Directly into her eyes. She seemed to be filling up. So sincere were her words that Joe actually understood most of what she said but still not sure how all this all exactly applied to him. "Mama," he said. "What is it you wantin' me to do? Just behave myself?"

"Nothing different, sweetheart. I just want you to know the secret. Yes, you behave, you study real good in high school, you work hard, and you are going to be a success in life. No one is going to tell you that you are a poor black kid with no chance in life getting ahead unless you are lucky enough to be singled out and handed your success. The secret sweetheart is called 'discipline'. It takes an effort to move ahead in life. That effort is control over your emotions, thinking before you act, acting wisely. That's all called 'self-discipline'. Your great grandfather Marvin learned it from his father and from the Army. He was really something. He was a success. The Army had lots of rules of behavior. That training, that discipline, was to teach how to be orderly in combat in order to succeed and for teaching self-discipline, to survive when things got tough."

The 'chat' was over for the evening. Mama seemed to be getting a little emotional, Joe mused. Maybe she was losing a little self-discipline herself, Joe laughed to himself, but nevertheless, her sincere talk gave him a renewed sense of purpose – he was going to head right to his bedroom and have the self-discipline to really work on those situps and push ups with renewed vigor.

—◊—

Joe had just finished his workout, and to himself he smiled at the window air conditioner blowing full blast. The night was hot and humid, but brother William had installed the best A/C unit that he could buy. He was still not sure exactly how William had all this money as Joe had not yet been informed exactly how all this drug business worked. At the playground the older guys traded for marijuana cigarettes and little packages of powders, but Joe had never been part of all that stuff nor yet offered anything. Maybe because they all knew that tricky business was little Joe's big brother's business.

Suddenly, to Joe's great surprise, William walked into the bedroom. It was so much earlier than when he usually came home, only 10 pm. He was in a sweat and had a troubled look on his face.

"Hey, what's up?" Joe asked with a quizzical look.

"Nothin' little brother" as he took off his nice bright blue long-sleeved shirt and sharp-looking trousers and put on a loose tee shirt, his face still looking sullen. Quite unusual, Joe thought to himself.

After a few moments of silence between the two, Joe spoke up. "Ya know, William, had dinner at Mama's again, and she keeps fillin' my ears with all kinds of stuff, bout me bein' good and all…. You gonna tell me bout all this drug stuff you do, how you get all this great stuff … shoes, clothes, watches, car rentals." His voice trailed off, his head bowed, as if now afraid that he finally brought this subject up to his big brother.

William slowly looked over at him and for the first time began to explain to his younger brother what his world was all about. Joe was sitting down on the edge of his bed directly across from William, He stretched out on his bed but facing towards Williams's bed. Their eyes did not meet.

"Joe, you are a good kid. I thought I was too at your age. But I learned a little too much in high school. I learned that we blacks had nowhere to go. A few kids, I guess the bright ones, or the lucky ones, got plucked out and got a free ride at some fancy high school, but the kids left at my school were rough, did not listen to the teachers or the so-called counselors. We argued, we fought, we fought with our fists, and some kids had knives and guns. Many kids dropped out of school, never graduatin'. What was I gonna to do if I stayed? There were no good jobs to turn to. Work for minimum wage at some food dump? Work driving a garbage truck for the stupid city, a janitor cleaning bathrooms, go in the Army and get killed? Or, or Joe, join the group controllin' our block, the drug gang making money. It was easy, it was an easy decision. I just had to follow orders and do my part getting the drugs from the delivery boys, be aware of the undercover cops, sellin' what I had for cash – packages of marijuana, cocaine, heroin to the drug users who would come to my street corner.... I make money, Joe, I make money." His voice trailed off.

A few moments of silence followed. William continued to sit still on the edge of his bed, looking down. Joe turned his face toward William's and finally spoke. "Okay, okay, I got it, but why you lookin' so down. You got it good, no?"

"Not so easy, little brother. It's a big system. We are a little gang in a big system. We control four corners on four blocks. Sixteen spots. But we are not alone. There are bigger gangs aways lookin' for more. There are older guys settin' the prices. Tonight, my group felt the sting. Our prices not keepin' up, our locations bein' threatened. My boss had a gun put in his face. He then pushes me to up our prices. Don't know, don't know ...." His voice trailing off again. Silence. Joe rested his head down on his pillow. It was the first time he learned what his older brother was doing every day and night, but now didn't want to hear any more. He could sense and feel his brother's anxiety. Joe had the sensation of helplessness. It did not feel good. He closed his eyes and hoped he would soon fall asleep.

# 3

Another great dinner, turkey, mashed potatoes, and string beans, with butter pecan ice cream for dessert. Of course, followed by Mama Sarah pointing Joe into the living room for another chat. This time, however, it was Joe who started the conversation. "Mama, I have to tell you somethin'. Today, on the playground, I got a little involved. Ya know, I'm getting stronger every day from my workouts, not even one week, but I really pushed a guy really hard after he tried to steal the ball from me and grabbed my arm. He's about sixteen, and he was about to throw a punch at me when my big friend pulled him back. Guess I'm understandin' what you talkin' bout ... behavior. That kid loses his cool, I lose my cool, but then my big friend comes to my rescue because he likes me on his side. I'm fast and I feed hm the ball.... Well, that was the end of that so-called 'conflict'. No violence. Mama."

Sarah sat back relaxed with a slight smile showing on her face. "Anymore, Joe?"

"Yeah, I understand a little more now bout drugs, you know, William's business, right. So I ask my friend how come some of the older kids at the playground sometimes are tradin' or sellin' drugs? I thought it was a corner business. So he tells me there are guys who can't afford the corner prices, and there are guys who want to sell some of theirs to make some extra money or even maybe they have stolen them. He told me you're just a kid, stay out of it. You're not going to be so fast if you start usin' them…. Mama, this is a big mess. Another kid tells me, 'when it gets tough, you have to be tougher, fight back harder than what hit you'. Geez!" Joe turned for a change to look at his great grandmother right into her eyes, unconsciously seeking her wisdom.

"Young Joe, my best guy, wow, you are learning fast. As they say 'life is not a bowl of cherries'. I guess this is why I try to talk to you so much. Life on this earth is not so easy. Some are born into wealth and an easy life, not that they are always happy with that. Most of us live in a never-ending struggle, but among us those who smartly use their own talents, their own merits, well, they live a life of fulfillment, of achievement, of personal accomplishment, and are the happiest. That's what I'm trying to get across to you Joe. Lots of roadblocks out there, lots of temporary shortcuts that don't pay off in time, lots of people who can lead you astray. We blacks came to this country as slaves, working hard for no reward. After two hundred years we were given our freedom, but for the next hundred years treated as second class citizens, but then finally given equal rights some sixty years ago. We became mayors and police chiefs in our big cities, important politicians like our first black president, members of Congress, TV personalities. But many of us remain right here where we are. As you know we are not starving, but many of us do not have great economic opportunities to succeed. We who are not prepared. What I'm trying to tell you is that despite your blackness, you stay orderly under the law, you learn real good in school, you work hard in everything you do, you will find opportunities, and you will advance on your merits. You will make something of yourself, and you will find self-satisfaction and personal dignity from that effort, that achievement, that accomplishment." Mama finally paused and took a deep breath, looked over at Joe to see if he was listening. She smiled, as she saw her great grandson looking at her intently. He was listening. His face was not questioning. He seemed to be understanding.

—⁓—

The next day, young Joe was on the basketball court by 10 a.m. After listening to brother William and Mama Sarah, he felt for the first time a sense of self-worth. Fooling around with drugs did not seem so attractive. I'll stay away from those playground gatherings he thought. And maybe I'll take a few shots the next game. What the heck. Effort, right?

For the next hour, there were only four kids on one end of the court with two balls, so Joe concentrated on taking and making 15-foot jump shots after dribbling the ball intently shifting one direction then another with his dribble and footwork. It seemed to be working. By 11 a.m. more kids showed up including the 17-year-old dominating big kid who loved having Joe on his team to feed him the ball. As usual the big kid called the players and the game. Joe and two others on his team, four against four, full court, twenty points by two baskets. At sixteen-sixteen, Joe at last felt his chance. He didn't have to think now, he just felt it. He adeptly stole the ball, then used his speed and dribbling ability to move swiftly down the court but instead of his usual pass to the big guy also speeding down the court, Joe pulled up at about 15 feet out and fired a jump shot. It missed and the ball fell into one of his opponent's hands who quickly hurled the ball to the other end of the court into the hands of his teammate who laid it in for an easy basket. The big guy, the kid Joe thought his friend, immediately fumed at Joe and shouted in anger.

"What the shit, man. Whatta you doin'? I was wide open. Why you take that crazy shot?" His glare at Joe was piercing.

Joe looked at him head bowed with a playground ball, historic, automatic answer. "Sorry, didn't see you." I screwed up he thought to himself. It got worse. The perturbed big guy missed his next shot. The other team made their next shot to win the game 20 to 16. As was the custom on this court, if there are four guys waiting to play, the winners stay on the court and the losers go off. Away to the side, the big guy laid into Joe again. In a firm strong voice of deep baritone, with all the kids on the playground not playing the current basketball game to hear, the big guy let Joe have it. "Listen little man, you are the young guy here. What fourteen and undersized? You get to play with us only because, man, you fast and you can dribble. We do the shootin'. We're out because you screwed up. You want to play again, you move and pass. You got that, little Joe?"

Joe felt shell shocked. He could feel his heart beating. He nodded sheepishly towards the big guy. His summer life was on that playground. He had nothing else to do. He sat down in the shade on the hard cement and reflected. I was making that shot when I came. It seemed the right thing to do. I didn't even look to see if the big guy was open or near. How did I miss and screw up? Effort and reward, what was Mama Sarah talkin' bout?

But **there was** a reward for effort, he soon learned. Continuing his increase in nightly situps and pushups, he sure did notice his gain in strength. Where it rapidly showed up was on that basketball court the next two weeks before the start of high school. The big guy continued to name fast Joe on his team. And while a submissive Joe took no shots, it was obvious the older players couldn't push him around to try to steal the ball from him. He could now use his elbows and shoulders and arms to push back to the point where the bigger guys didn't even want to mess around with him anymore. He seemed to command a new respect. Most rewarding – as the summer all day season was closing and the guys said Saturdays now would be game day, the big guy said to Joe in an surprisingly friendly tone of voice: "Little Joe, I be playin' varsity my senior year, maybe even lookin' for a college scholarship. You made me look good here this summer, boy. There were some college scouts here. I'm telling you to keep practicing, learn to shoot good, and go out for our freshmen bball team. Got it little guy ... strongman?"

Joe was speechless, but his eyes lite up as he nodded affirmative. He felt a sense of pride. He was learning the good feeling of self-confidence, of strong effort paying off.

## 4

"Up Joe, let's go. Seven o'clock. You cannot be late for school your first day. Get dressed and come down for breakfast. You have to leave quarter to eight."

"Mom ... geez," Joe replied grudgingly. But with a shake of his head, he was fully awake and quickly rose from his bed. Right to the floor for some situps and pushups. William's bed was empty, not unusual. At his breakfast of cereal, a hardboiled egg, buttered toast and orange juice, he felt a mixture of happy anticipation and nervous anxiety. Hard to describe exactly. His first day of high school, a school full of neat kids, making new friends, an all-new experience, but a school with a reputation for having some very tough kids, rowdy kids, metal detectors at the doors, cops on duty in the hallways, doors locked at a certain time. And Mama Sarah's warnings.

"My goodness, son. That shirt does not fit you very well. I'll have a new one for you tomorrow," Mom Ella blurted out. "Guess I forgot. At fourteen you boys grow fast. Joe, you look taller and bigger than what you were just couple weeks ago. A real growth spurt." But Joe looked up from the breakfast table directly at his mom and instantly changed the thought to *I like this shirt tight. It's showing my muscle strength in just three weeks from all my pushups.*

Finishing up his breakfast and looking down again he could barely hear her last words. "Now Joe, I know this is a big day for you. Your first day in high school. Let me tell you it may be a little rough and rowdy, but you pay attention and learn somethin', ya' hear me son?" Joe gave an automatic quick nod, but then gave her words a little more thought. *Sounds just like Mama Sarah,* and he suddenly felt a sense of excitement.

Right on his mom's departure time at 7:45, Joe set out for his ten-minute walk to his new high school. She had given him a new backpack to put on, containing two pencils, a note pad and the letter from the school indicating he would be reporting by 8 o'clock each morning to Room 9 on the second floor as his home room. It also read to enter by only the main front door in order to pass through security. By chance, Joe bumped into his best friend from junior high school as the two approached the crowded front door of the high school, a rather massive building in Joe's eyes, a red brick building with lots of windows on its five floors. Charles had spent the summer at the shore with his mother, brothers and sisters so Joe had not seen or heard from him in a couple of months. Charles was definitely taller, Joe noticed immediately, but still quite thin. He was holding a cell phone in his hand, like so many other kids of similar age. While William's cash income could certainly have bought a cell phone for Joe, Mom Ella forbade it and pushed Joe to spend his summer active on the basketball court and not sitting around playing video games and on social media. "Plen-dy time for that ahead Joe," she had decreed.

"Hey bro, what's up. Good summer? Ya look strong, man," Charles said with a slight punch to Joe's arm.

"Yeah, Charles. Hot up here all summer. Worked on my basketball game. Gonna go out for the freshman team." By good coincidence Charles had the same home room assignment as Joe. After finding and entering Room 9 on the second floor, the two sat down in adjoining seats while most of the other kids were talking loudly standing up.

A big clock on the front wall above the blackboard read 8:03 when a middle-aged woman, white skin, rather thin, with her black hair back in a bun entered the room and commanded "sit, sit." She proceeded to the black board and wrote in large printed letters MRS LONGMIRE. One of the many still standing boys shouted out "Mrs. Longcrap?" Most of the kids, still standing, broke out in a huge laugh. Without changing the serious look on her face, she proceeded to sit down at her desk and spoke clearly and firmly. "When you all get tired of talking and standing, ya'll will sit down and I'll take roll. I'm just your homeroom teacher, not your disciplinarian. You skip school or come in real late, that's your problem not mine." Her voice was strong enough for all to hear despite the ongoing laughter and chatter that by now was substantially subsiding. Joe had remained quiet through this whole introduction. Mrs. Longmire read through the names in alphabetical order and the kids' responses were of a great variety of "here, yeah, missing in action, maybe, presently, yesum," but the room was full so it appeared to Joe that everyone was present at least on this first day, and it seemed to Joe that the girls in this classroom compared to the boys were much more orderly through this process than the boys. Joe then thought that this teacher remained so calm that she must have gone through this many times before. After rollcall, she stood up and walked down the two aisles front to back passing out a single piece of paper to each student while stating loud and clear: "This is your course schedule and their room numbers and your teachers. When you hear the bell at eight thirty, you go.... It was nice meeting you all." She seemed to have a slight grin on her face as she returned up front to her desk and the students' noises began again at a loud pitch.

Joe studied the writing on the paper with his name on top closely – the days, times, room numbers or gym, the teachers, and all the subjects as well as two recesses and lunch period. Dismissal every day at 3 p.m. English, math, history and biology every day, gym twice a week, art once a week, music once a week, health once a week, study hall every day. Compared to junior high, this sure looked challenging to

Joe, but remembering his Mama Sarah's and his mother's encouragement, this is all going to be exciting.

—◁◁◁—

His first two classes were really neat, Joe thought. English and math. The teachers introduced themselves and passed out respective textbooks. A lot of consistent chatter among the students, but Joe had been warned about that and thought no bother. The short walk between classrooms along crowded hallways was exciting. A big, crowded, noisy movement of kids of all sizes, kinds of dress and even skin colors. Most kids were black but some were light brown, Asian, and even a few whites. Joe thought interesting but certainly not alarming in any sense. That aspect was all to come later.

To Joe's thinking it was great that his long-time friend Charles was alongside him in this new experience. After the second class, the paper instruction sheet showed a fifteen-minute recess. Now the hallways were really bustling, some kids running downstairs and out an open but security guarded back door to a fenced in yard, some kids rushing in and out of the "Boys" "Girls" bathrooms. Joe and Charles just wandered slowly along the second floor hallways towards their next classroom until Charles was stopped and confronted by a larger kid, face to face.

The bigger kid wore a tight tee shirt revealing quite a strong muscular frame. To Joe, his facial expression looked mean, serious. He had long black hair tied in a knot behind his neck and shoulders. He had indeterminable tattoos in various colors on both arms from his wrists up.

"Hey, you, kiddo. Ain't you Tony James' little brother? Charles?" Charles looked bewildered but gave a brief nod affirmative. "He here in school?"

"No, dropped out, last year," Charles replied weakly.

"Right, man. So where you two been all summer? I been lookin'."

"Yeah, down the shore, both workin' there."

"Ya'll home now?'

"Yeah, yeah, we're home."

The big kid stepped back a pace but continued to look right into Charles eyes as he spoke, still tough and mean as Joe witnessed in awe. Charles seemed frozen in place.

"Okay, kiddo. Your brother still owes me $500 from last May and then he whoosh, gone. He never answers his cell phone neither. I go to your house and no one answers the door. At the shore, huh, well I'll be over tonight.... Must have made some dough down there, right? He better have it, kiddo." With that, he gave Charles a light fist pump into his chest and turned away, disappearing as fast as he appeared.

Joe felt confused. "What was that all 'bout, Charles? That guy really looked tough, bro'"

"Yeah, Eddie, from the next block from us. Don't know. My brother won't talk 'bout what he does. He was real good at the shore this summer. Had a good job parkin' cars for a big restaurant. Don't know, Joe. He may be in drug dealing up here like I know your brother is. Know that's where the big money is. He won't tell us why he dropped out of school every time my mom asks him. Com'on, let's go."

The third class was history. The teacher, a large looking middle-aged black man well overweight with big eyeglasses and graying short hair started by shouting "quiet down" as he walked down the aisles passing out large textbooks. The big letters on the front spelled 'World History'. The classroom drew far from quiet as he next roared out: "This year, you get this – World History, including history of Africa. Next year you get American History, including history of slavery, junior year you get European History, whites and Hispanics. Hang 'round you people, this is all important stuff." Raising his voice even more now, he spoke out quite firmly: "Gotta know where you came from 'fore you know where ya goin'". His voice was so bold now the kids suddenly quieted down. "My name is up on the blackboard there. Mister Washington, Ron Washington."

With the buzz in the classroom renewing, and with some kids in the back up and down, Joe did not know it yet but besides his great grandmother, Mama Sarah, Mr. Washington was to soon become the most inspirational person in young Joe

Robinson's life. Onward, to the fourth class of the morning, Biology. Up on the third floor, lab benches were situated in the science classrooms. Joe thought this subject would be very interesting to him as he knew nothing about the world of what living creatures are all about. Repeating the earlier morning classes, there was no beginning learning, just the passing out of textbooks, teacher introductions, and a lot of noises, student movements, laughter, and chatter. As there had been no 'teaching time' or scuffles or violent acts yet, Joe was assuming Mama Sarah's 'lack of discipline' would start tomorrow when the teaching and learning would begin.

Nevertheless, the one-hour lunch period was chaotic. Some kids brought lunch boxes, pails, or bags to school. Others had some money to buy items in the side counters in the cafeteria. Some put coins into the vending machines to buy snacks and sodas. Joe had nothing and thought that his Mom had assumed the high school kids got free lunches like the grade school kids did. Seeing Joe's shortcoming, Charles had four extra quarters that he passed on to Joe, who then ended up with two packages of fig bars and a Pepsi from one of the several vending machines. Finding an adjoining seat next to Charles, Joe noticed the older boys sat down together at the long, large tables while girls of any age also sat together. Seemed quite natural to Joe, but what amazed him was that he thought high school would show a little more maturity than the constant yelling like went on back in grade school and junior high. "Charles, I can hardly hear you," is about all Joe could get out to his best friend sitting next to him. Disorderly, like Mama had warned but at least no fighting.

The once a week after lunch class this first day was Art. The classroom was set up with large, long tables so that each student would have space to draw or paint, similar to the cafeteria tables but with chairs, not benches. Again, the time was filled with teacher introduction, and instead of a textbook a folder was passed out containing various sketches and color paintings. The teacher pointed out where various pens, pencils, brushes, and paint tubes were assembled in the front of the classroom. But again, no teaching or learning took place on this first day of high school. Joe felt all this okay for the first day, getting organized, and he only seemed perturbed by the constant movement and chatter of so many of the kids, his new classmates.

The last so-called class was "Study Hall" but obviously no one opened one single one of the books they received earlier that day despite the so-called teacher there constantly begging the kids to quiet down, open a book, and read one of their first assignments. Joe followed the herd, never opening a book, just quizzing Charles about what he was going to do after school. A remarkable first day of school for Joe Robinson, disorderly but not fearsome. His feelings of anxiety and excitement turned to the anticipation of classroom learning and whether or not that was really possible in this environment.

—⁓—

Engaged in all the lively activity outside the school building soon after the last school bell rang, where everyone seemed to have nosily rushed, not walked, out the doors, Joe shouted out enthusiastically "see ya tomorrow Charles" and jogged home to his room so he could resume his strength building exercise program. After seeing all those bigger kids in the school hallways and all the pushing and shoving, he was now feeling, not intimidated, but doubly motivated to get bigger and stronger. It was now not just about basketball.

That evening at dinner with his mother Ella and sister Etta, he received a barrage of questions from them inquiring as to how his first day of high school went. He simply kept replying "okay" "fine" "good" with no further elaboration. He did not want to admit it all seemed rather chaotic. He then wondered if he should open any of the textbooks he was given by his various teachers, but before he could reach a decision, the front door unlocked and in came Mama Sarah, a big smile on her face. She was still so pretty and attractive even at age 85 Joe mused. Really, my best friend, he felt inside.

"So, my boy, how did your big first day go at that awesome high school?"

"Okay, Mama, okay," he quickly replied with a slight nod. "No big conflicts," he smiled. Then he remembered the big kid who had confronted Charles in the hallway.

"Meet any good-looking young ladies, did you?" Joe just looked down with a slight grin and shook his head negative.

"Well, you soon will, my boy, and you just remember you treat those ladies with respect, you know what I mean, no cussing, no hands on. Don't know what they will be teaching you there Joe, but boys and girls your age have it all you know? You know your family Joe, and I pray you are going to be more responsible, more disciplined. You make no babies until you and that beautiful young girl are both ready. You understanding me?"

Joe had the look again of 'what the heck is she talking about now?' but it was okay; this was his idol speaking. Mama's granddaughter and great granddaughter were still sitting at the dining room table hearing all these commands, but they sat still with blank looks on their faces. Joe had the thought that Mama's lecture was intended for them as well. Maybe to vent. She could not be happy that this pair had no or little idea who the responsible fathers were in their disruptive lives.

# 5

The next morning at breakfast with his mom, there were no words. It was like his mother was still upset with Mama Sarah bursting in the night before and delivering a moral lecture. Upon Joe's departure, she finally uttered, without looking at him "I packed a sandwich and a drink for you in your backpack. Have a good day, as they say."

"Bye Mom," and he was out the door. Again, he bumped into Charles shortly before entering the school grounds. Charles was looking down as he walked along side, looking very grim. "What's up, bro? You lookin' mean, boy." Joe had the thought that it was still hot and humid the end of August, and maybe Charles didn't have air conditioning in his bedroom or maybe if he did it wasn't working.

"Shit, man. Last night. My father, he didn't show up at the shore all summer. Last night my mother wasn't spectin' him, and he shows up for dinner. Christ, all they did was argue. He wants to know where she is getting' all this money. She took an apartment at the shore, buys all this food. She dare not tell him their son Tony, my brother, has drug connections and makes some big side money. She just says she's saved it up.... He eats, he leaves, thought he was going to bop her on the chin. He's done it before.... Shit, man."

"Sonna bitch, bro, that's crazy." Joe didn't know what else to say.

"That's not all. Gets worse, man. That kid Eddie, told ya bout yesterday after he came up to us in the hall. He shows up, bout 9 o'clock. Pounds on the door and yells "Hey Tony, you home, man?" Tony and me, watchin' tv, Phillies game, in the livin' room. My brother let's 'im in. Crazy. Eddie demands his money. My brother says he ain't got it. Give me another week. Eddie, pretty big bastard. He just throws a left punch into my brother's stomach and then a right into my brother's face, says, 'get the money, man, see ya next week'."

The pair were now at the crowded front door of their school building getting in line to pass through the metal detectors and finish passing through security. The chatter from all the surrounding kids was so loud that Joe could not even respond to Charles to ask how his brother is doing after that altercation with Eddie.

Throughout that day, Charles seemed remote, detached as the two went together through their classroom changes subject to subject. At lunch, Joe did have the chance to ask Charles how his brother was doing after that unexpected attack. Charles remained despondent as he replied with a simple "really hurtin'." For Joe, the school day seemed a disappointment in ways hard to describe. He had difficulty putting a clear meaning to it. He had thought sure first day would be a little chaotic – new teachers, new kids from different junior highs, getting organized into different classroom locations, getting textbooks, making new friends, lots of talk, lots of noise. On this second day many of the kids seemed very attentive, well behaved, but still there were quite a few who seemed to have little or no interest in learning, and some quite disruptive. He did understand this school was not one of those charter schools around which there was so much controversy or one of those special or private schools where the smart or rich kids go, or where certain kids somehow get picked out and receive special treatment. This was his school where most of the kids in his neighborhood were destined to attend. Then he thought briefly of his older brother and sister, both dropouts, never finishing high school and neither one getting a high school degree. He had never previously inquired about their reasons for dropping out although he now understood the lure of drug money and the unintended pregnancy. He could not quite fathom why it seemed in every class there were kids, mostly boys, in the back of the room mostly standing, mostly talking, despite their teachers' requests to sit down and be quiet. Joe's inner feelings were a complex mix of enthusiasm and despair. *I like this. I don't like this.*

That evening after dinner, Joe took it on his own to go next door to Mama Sarah and seek her out for some answers. She welcomed him and beckoned to sit on her couch together. "You know, my boy, it's all so very complicated. But you remember I started to tell you about conflict. Joe, it's part of who we are. It's a big part of what we call human nature, the way we act, the way we behave. Sometimes good, sometimes bad, whichever at the moment that seems to be to our advantage. When you study your history, going all the way back thousands of years, you will see war, war, war; conquer, conquer, conquer; fighting, fighting, fighting, and all that is still going on around the world today. You know, that's between kingdoms, nations, peoples, but it's also between individuals, persons. Joe, no two brains are alike; we are all each slightly different person to person. It could be differences in our genetic makeups, our histories from the time of inception, our environments, our chemistries in our brains, our hormones in our bodies, how many brain cells we have and how they are functioning, what we have been taught, who has influenced us the most. I know, I'm confusing you; you haven't even learned biology or psychology yet, but the point is, the nature of humans is that many of us are born disorderly, the reason why I told you before we need laws, rules, to be good and not bad. Joe, this all takes discipline, and I think what you are seeing in your high school in just two days is the lack of discipline, someone enforcing how you behave. Those kids you're talking about come to school without discipline, and the poor teachers there can't enforce it, can't control it. There is no penalty for being unruly, undisciplined or if there is, there's no way to enforce a punishment.

"But Mama, you keep tellin' me I'm a good boy. Here I don't know who my father is. He sure ain't givin' me discipline. My mom's super nice. She don't say much, not like you do. My brother and sister both dropped out of school... why I'm good?"

"Joe, Joe, listen, so far, you're a natural. But first thing we are going to do is correct your English. You pay attention and try to learn to speak clearly and with correct English, like I'm going to try with you right now. You remember how disorderly your kindergarten and first grade were – nobody paying attention to the teachers. I tried then to help you read and write good English, but I don't think I tried hard enough. Let's start getting it right, including putting a 'g' at the end of our words ending in 'ing', no more 'ain't', no more 'yeahs'." Mama Sarah sat back and smiled, but quickly sat up and got serious again. "Your brother and sister, you could be like them too. You know, you are going to be influenced by a bunch – by your classmates, by the kids you play with, the kids you associate with, by the quality of the teachers you have, by what you watch on tv, by what you read, by this social media stuff you kids get into, by your coach and teammates if you play on the basketball team at school, and I pray to the good Lord above, you are also influenced by me. And yes, I am telling you, you are a good boy. Are you going to still be a good boy in four years as you graduate from high school and go on to college, or a good skilled job, or our national service in the military?" Mama Sarah sat back on the couch after she delivered that sermon wondering if any of that got through to her great-grandson, who sat still in silence and looking a little bewildered.

—◊◊◊—

The new school year began on a Thursday, so it was only two days of the high school experience for Joe before it was basketball weekend at the nearby playground. As before, the big kid chose Joe to be on his team, but this time another tall, well-built player, named Garner, gathered enough courage to challenge the big kid as to why he always chose Joe, the fast kid who dribbled the ball well and always fed the ball to the big kid to shoot, and that team almost never lost a game.

"What's it to ya, man. Just shut up and play the game. Twenty by two. Winner stays on," replied the big kid sharply, clearly. Garner backed off. The first game of the day went to the big guy and Joe and the two other teammates, who were mostly rebounders and occasional shooters when they had an open shot. The big kid scored fourteen of their twenty points. This time Garner did not back down.

"That kid there who just runs and passes you the ball all

the time, why you force him on your team all the time? We should alternate choosin' just like we do everybody else."

"I told ya, man. Just shut your mouth and wait til you get on the court 'gain." The two antagonists were almost of equal size with Garner slightly smaller in height and muscle appearance. But Garner had now gained some courage, or was it a misguided emotion, to take the big kid on. They stood face to face staring into each other's eyes. The big kid gave Garner a slight push in the chest, "Off the court, you got next game."

Garner tensed and pushed the big guy back in the chest. That was it. Joe watched in awe as all hell broke loose. Fists flew, arms locked, both went to the hard cement. Then suddenly to the advantage of the big kid now kneeling above Garner, who was now face up with his back on the ground, the big kid threw a number of hard punches right into Garner's face, who screamed loudly as the big kid quickly stood up over his antagonist, fists clenched. He was now definitely the king of this playground, that is if all fights were to be settled only by fisticuffs.

Joe had a difficult time focusing the rest of the day and seemed to be playing all the remaining games by rote memory. He felt completely exhausted by 4 o'clock, thirsty and hot on this very warm day. Told the big guy he had errands to do at home for his mother and had to leave. The big guy just nodded to him and gave him an approving tap on the top of his head. All the way back home, Joe kept thinking about what Mama Sarah had been saying to him about conflict. That sure was it, the violent kind.

Sunday night's dinner was not much better as far as disputes, but at least no violence. It was Sunday, and as usual on that day, Mom had invited Beatrice and Sarah over as well. Even William made the big Sunday dinners. A real family affair. A nice mixed salad, pot roast with mashed potatoes and warm string beans, but before the apple pie and ice cream dessert could be served on this Sunday, someone had to again bring up the subject of Etta's pregnancy. It was MomMom Beatrice: "So Etta, what's you doin' bout that baby. Abort or keep?" Quite blunt was the tone. The table went silent for a moment while all eyes went to Etta's.

"Jesus, MomMom, what the...." Sixteen-year-old Etta sure did not expect this subject to come up in the middle of the family's routine Sunday dinner. It was usually afterwards. All eyes continued their stares at this very pretty young girl, who despite her awkward situation, continued to dress well, apply her makeup perfectly, and fix her hair almost professionally. Older than Joe and no longer in school, she was granted the time and freedom by her mom to enjoy all her social media sites, and Joe surmised that's how she spent 80% of her day. Etta finally ended the silence around the table. "I still think I want to have this baby. It's a human being, a real person growing and developing inside of me. I want to love it, raise it, and give it, him or her, a real chance to do better in life than I've done so far with myself." She looked up rather proud of herself that she got that statement out. But Mom Ella and grandmother MomMom Beatrice did not share her exuberance. Beatrice did not waste a moment to speak up.

"Etta, you crazy, girl. You just too young to be makin' that decision. You look at us. Your mother and grandmother, you and your brother Joe, livin' off your Mom's little salary, some government handouts, some extra money from brother William here. No men, no fathers, 'round here payin' us nothin'. Don't bring your kid into our world. Not right."

Joe listened to this debate go on for quite a while, delaying his joy of having the coming dessert, and with Mama Sarah just nodding to him with her eyes saying to him 'See, told you so, on and on, this world of conflict.'

Later that night, after his now routine grinding floor exercises, his bathroom duties, checking out William's empty bed, setting his alarm clock for an early morning rise, and turning off his bedside light, Joe felt himself wide awake. He thought about getting back to school the next morning and wondered about whether things would get more orderly there, but foremost in his mind was Mama Sarah's explanations about conflict. In just the last couple of days, there is his best friend's brother getting punched out over a money dispute, his friend the big kid on the basketball court punching out another kid over a dispute about over who he, Joe, should be playing with, and then the family argument whether Etta should have this baby or abort it. Maybe, I hope, tomorrow in school, we'll just have noise but no fighting.

But it would not take long for that thought to be shattered.

# 6

Again, Joe met up with Charles shortly before reaching the high school main entrance, and again Charles seemed perturbed.

"Hey bro, com'on, things no better at home?" Joe inquired.

"Nah," Charles readily replied staring down at the ground as they walked side by side among the growing crowd of noisy kids. "My stupid brother told our father 'bout gettin' punched to explain his swollen face but didn't tell him why, so now the two of them workin' out a way to get back at that kid Eddie. Shit, man, stupid assholes. That kid Eddie must have big connections." Joe just stared at Charles speechless. What, he thought, could he offer?

The homeroom attendance taking was just like the first two days - lots of wisecracks and Mrs. Longmire seeming to ignore the chatter and seeming to be secretly smiling underneath it all. Like just doing her job in the most minimal way possible. After all, this was not a learning class. On the other hand, Joe's first two classes, English and Math, were to be learning classes, but both entailed enough disorderliness that both teachers appeared frustrated in their repeated attempts for full attention from those at the back of the classrooms. It seemed that if a student wanted to pay attention and learn something, then sit in the front half of the classroom, exactly where Joe ended up. But it disturbed Joe that friend Charles seemed distracted and went to the back and sat quietly among those who were up and down and constantly talking.

The third class was quite different - History with Mr. Washington. He started by clapping his hands vigorously and shouting "Ya all know where ya came from?" Amazingly, this approach produced quiet all the way to the back of the classroom. Then changing his tone and volume to a nice clear calm sound, he said as he stood around to the front of his desk: "Well by golly this World History course is going to teach you all just that, and when you learn that, you will then understand where you are and where you are going." The 9th grade kids actually listened to him. Joe felt excited about what was going on in this classroom. Finally, an exception to Mama Sarah's conflict chats!

But that good feeling dissipated quickly at lunchtime in the cafeteria. He had a difficult time getting Charles to converse with him, or with anyone else. Charles was obviously despondent over his brother's recent violent encounter with that kid Eddie. Suddenly, unexpectedly, Charles jumped up from the table halfway through his sandwich and started across the room at a fast clip. In a flash, he was at the table of the bigger, older kids, and Joe could clearly see that Charles was throwing punches at, yes, they were towards Eddie. Much bigger than 14 year old Charles, who although had grown much taller the last few months was still quite thin. It was obvious that Eddie successfully deflected the surprise blows from Charles, and then rising quickly to his feet, he took and landed one big punch squarely into Charles nose, who screamed and went streaming to the floor. Other kids who had been sitting by Eddie quickly rose and restrained him from behind before he could do more damage to young Charles, who had obviously lost his cool. Suddenly, the noisy lunchroom went strangely quiet while two teachers rushed over, held up their hands to caution Eddie to retreat, then leaned down to help Charles up. His nose was bleeding, and one of the teachers grabbed and handed him some napkins to hold to his nose. Without thinking of the rationale behind this sudden event, Joe rushed over and offered "I'm his friend. I'll take him." The two teachers nodded affirmative. Escorting Charles by the arm out of the turmoil and out of the lunchroom, which very quickly resumed its usual loud vocal sounds, Joe could now put his rational thoughts together. "Charles, I know you're upset about this guy Eddie and his involvement with your brother Tony, but you can't lose your cool, bro. The kid is big and strong. You lost your head for a good cause, but there is a better way to get back at him. Com'on, I'm walking you home, the heck with the rest of the day here."

It had taken only three days of Joe's attendance before the heralded violence took place at his new high school, and here, thought Joe, it's right with my best friend. *Am I involved too? What do I do now?* The walk to Charles home, a few blocks past Joe's home was now one of open conversation. Charles could express himself again. Joe cautioned "Bro, that kid is too big and strong, must have a lot of connections. Let's keep your father out of it...."

"My brother has a gun. We can shoot the bastard," Charles interrupted, speaking clearly and sternly now, still holding a napkin to his nose. "Probably broke my nose, that son of a bitch."

"No, no," Joe replied quickly and forcefully. 'Member, Charles, he's probably part of a gang. Have more guns than you do. And I'm not lettin' you go to youth detention for years for committin' murder. No way, bro. Must be a better way." Arriving at Charles doorstep, the two had not come up with a solution, next step or a plan. "See ya at school 'morrow mornin'," Joe said as the two looked at each in the eyes and tapped their two clenched fists together. "Keep your mother and father out of this too, don't hurt your family, and stay 'way from Eddie, ya hear me?" was Joe's parting advice. But there was no acknowledgement of Joe's commands from Charles.

That evening after dinner, it was Joe's turn to seek out and have a chat with his great grandmother. She could sense his distress after they sat down together in her living room. "Geez, Mama, this isn't what I 'spected ... sorry, expected. Yes, I thought the older kids would be havin' ... having, fights at recess outside and maybe cussing the teachers in my classrooms, but Charles is my best friend, from back in grade school. Now, he's got a messed-up family with his brother in some kind of trouble, owing some tough kid some money, an older kid, a big tough kid in school with us. Charles, he lost his head today, got punched down at lunchtime in the cafeteria today. I walked him home, and he even thought about shooting the big kid. Whatta we do mama?"

Mama Sarah reached over and put her hand on Joe's thigh, patting lightly. "Joe, this is what we have been talking about." Her voice was calm, her words enunciated clearly, perfectly. This is exactly what you have to expect and deal with, even with your closest friends. You are going to learn fast. Look at the TV shows, look at the movies on TV, look at the fighting sports with men and women now, punching with little gloves, not boxing gloves, but kicking to the face, punching even when their opponent is down on the mat, look at the video games your friends play on their cell phones – violence. You see Joe, violence sells. The majority of movies have a V rating. As I explained to you, it's a basic part of our human nature. But we have to control it in real life, Joe, so it's only for entertainment. It's too bad we have certain people who lose it and have to do violence in real life, to settle a score, to take an advantage, a number of selfish or unthinking reasons. What I am trying to get across to you is to get quickly past your emotional responses, think and reflect, allow your rational, reasonable part of your brain to takeover your actions. Your friend lost his cool. He was thinking emotionally, then acting irrationally. How was he going to win a fight in the cafeteria against a bigger, older kid? How is he going to help his brother without hurting himself by shooting the bigger kid? What I want you to learn is that you are constantly going to be faced with conflict situations, big and small, important and some not so important, but if you are going to be somebody in this world, you will find ways to resolve these conflicts without resorting to violence."

That outpouring from Mama Sarah was long winded, but Joe listened to her intently, staring at her calm face the whole time. He got the message. But he now wanted to pursue more with her, challenge her, as well as understand her. "Okay Mama, but the great grandfather I never knew, your Marvin, he went into the fighting military. We have all these countries with big armies, fighting here and there, we have all these murders, stealing, robberies with guns, so violence is a lot more than just a movie, TV entertainment. Right? It's not just us unruly kids. It's real life." Joe sat back, almost proud of himself he got that out.

"Right on, my boy, you got it. Like I have said to you over and over, we all can be born unruly, disorderly, and that behavior can show up at any time. That's part of who we are. So, every country, here every state, every city, has rules, laws, to try to keep us orderly so life can function for the good of the most. That's why we have religions, police, why we have judges and courts. Where we live is on the poorer side of America. Here we live with more than local jobs, like your mom; we do get government help like food stamps, but we are still considered the underclass because we have poorer houses, a lack of nearby higher paying jobs, more unemployment, nearby homeless, teenagers and young men stealing. Drugs, crime, guns, worse here. Your bad luck, your bad circumstances Joe, growing up here? But Joe, I want you to understand that millions and millions of we blacks have progressed, in the military, in the government, in professional sports, in the business world. Despite your disruptions in school and even on your playground, and despite you living here in this neighborhood, if you learn your schoolwork, if you work hard at whatever you do now and later on, you will be a success in this country. You will have the opportunities to do want you want to do. You just keep your cool, young man. Think before you act." Mama sat back and now looked like she needed a break. Quite a sermon. Joe nodded, reached over and gave her a kiss on her cheek. A warm inner feeling came over him. He then rose quietly and knew it was now time for his next set of exercises. For sure, he was going to work harder than ever at that.

# 7

Joe spent the rest of that school week with three things in mind – trying to calm down his good friend Charles, paying attention to Mr. Washington in World History class, and steadily increasing the number of situps and pushups before school, after school, and before bedtime.

At least Charles had become talkative again with Joe and their other classmates, even amicable, but periodically he would mention to Joe that he, his brother Tony, and their father were still discussing different ways to deal with the aggressive Eddie. Each time, Joe would insert his "no violence bro, no violence, will just get you into trouble." Charles would just smirk in return.

Mr. Washington seemed to have a unique way of holding his entire class's attention. His voice was bold and clear certainly, and he paced the front of the classroom with an air of authority, but he also was getting his subject matter across. "So 'ya all had some chicken last night for dinner, or maybe a meat ball, along with some turnips? Well folks, 'ya know we all been around for couple hundred thousand years huntin', fishin', finding berries and nuts off the trees, 'ya know – cave men. Then 'bout twelve thousand years ago, some ten thousand years before Jesus, we had the so-called Agricultural Revolution. Write that down, may be on your first test. We had some folks who learned how to grow crops, like wheat, and they learned how to domesticate some animals like cows and goats, chickens. So they didn't have to go out huntin' as much, so some sat around and learned how to communicate better with a fuller language and then to write, and to think about and record things in a better way. Folks this is what we call the dawn of Civilization, yeah, man from Ancient History to Civilization. Took a while, but eventually we understand now that we developed bigger tribes, societies, where the strong man became the leader over the others and that some learned men began to explain the reason for certain natural things, like they must be due to the supernatural, the gods. These leaders became the kings, lords, emperors, high priests. They became so smart and powerful, they learned they could increase their wealth, their goods, their power over others by using that inherited trait of aggressiveness to conquer others and gain their goods. So, we had the brown skinned Persian Empire, then the Egyptian Empire, the yellow skinned Mongolian Empire and various Chinese, the white skinned Greeks and Romans, all the way to the Europeans, Nazi Germany, Communist Russia and China, and then you guys see on TV today the Iranian and North Korean leaders ruling over their peoples.... Now I went a little fast here, but all this is going to be covered in detail in your text books. You guys are going to read all this, 'ya got it?

"And we are going to talk about Black history too. And how the more advanced folks with their technology, the Europeans, went into Africa where the native peoples there were less advanced in their societies, and the Europeans established colonies there in order to bring out goods they wanted back home. This time period was truly white supremacy, and then we'll go into the worldwide slave labor market that resulted from that."

Mr. Washington didn't have any time left for any questions from his students, but as the end of class bell rang, he sensed the almost bewildered look on the faces of almost all his students. He ended by saying "Tomorrow, I want each of you to ask me a question about what I discussed today. Got it?" Amazing, and to Joe gratifying, that at that moment Mr. Washington had the full attention of each and every student in that classroom.

—◊◊◊—

Late Friday afternoon, after a couple of basketball games at the playground court, Joe was back in his bedroom doing sets of situps and pushups with the air conditioner at full blast, when to his surprise brother William came in, sat down quickly on Joe's bed, and started to talk to him, actually looking at him right in the eye. "Little brother, stop a minute, listen up. I been thinkin', my life is gettin' a little messed up. In 'nother year, I was gonna teach you how to make some money in the drug dealin' business like me, but it's gettin' a little dane-dress. Listen, I got somethin' better for you. Nine clock tonight, 'bout fifty of us gonna hit the CVS store. Any kids caught, let go, no charges." He paused.

Joe looked up at his older brother and wandered what in the world is he talking about. William coughed and continued. "Listen, shopliftin' no big deal now. We take what we want for ourselves, but we take bags and grab other stuff too. We got a guy we meet later, takes that stuff and pays us money. They tell me some Mexican guy has the money, makes the payments, and takes the stuff. Somethin' 'bout Mexican cartels…. Look, I'm not into this myself. I got enough goin' on. I can take you tonight, but I got friends who can take you around and teach you the ropes. Joe, listen to me, you can make some money without getting' into the drug mess I'm in." Joe sat up flabbergasted, a blank look on his face. He did not answer his brother. He couldn't manage a clear thought. He remained speechless as William stood up and left the room. The two did not speak at all during dinner with Mom and Etta.

At 8:30 Joe was back on their bedroom floor when William entered and said, "Let's go." Joe felt empty of a response to his older brother, but automatically got up, put back on his shirt, and obediently followed William out.

The scene at the CVS store was chaotic, but somehow exhilarating for all those participating. A horde of teenage kids, boys and girls, noisily moving at breakneck speed through the aisles grabbing all kinds of goods, hustling out the doors, redshirted employees standing aside, helpless and in awe. A cop car swooping up outside with two policemen grabbing and restraining a couple of kids. Alongside his brother William, Joe copied him, put whatever was on the shelves in front of him into his black backpack, and quickly and safely followed William out. Swiftly away from the screaming mob. An hour later and blocks away from the mass shoplifting, with William directing, the pair met up with a large group of teenagers circled around three well-dressed men in an alley. All the kids turned over their bags to the men who had the tailgate lifted in their nearby SUV. The men shifted the contents of the bags into their SUV and then announced in an accent somewhat foreign to Joe. "No price for individual stuff you got. No time to pay you for how much each of you got. We pay you each same 'mount of cash tonight, but looka. You no have to do this mass thing like tonight. Too much attention. You each take what you can, by yourselves, when you can. We come different spot every Friday night. You will get the word where. We pay you each for what you got." The teenagers were dead quiet through all this exchange as no need to attract attention from nearby residents, and the three men seemed deadly serious as they spoke.

On the way home, William spoke first. "He was right. Don't be part of this mass thing. Too crazy. I just wanted to show you what it's all about. You can do this quietly on your own, drug stores, Wawa, Seven Eleven. You get experience, other retail stores. But be careful 'bout jewelry stores. They got lots security devices. Wear a hat or a hoody so any store cameras don't identify you."

Joe cut him off. "I don't know big brother. I don't know if I want to be breaking the law. I have to think about this." He just spoke perfect English. His mind switched to Mama Sarah. 'Enunciate clearly, speak good English, think before you act, you are a good boy'. This stealing just doesn't seem to make me feel good even though it's exciting.

# 8

The second full week in school was no less chaotic than the first week had been, except for Mr. Washington's class. A group of boys, although at times including some girls, were constantly disruptive. They mostly were towards the back of the classrooms. They simply seemed not wanting to learn anything. After all of Mama Sarah's 'chats', Joe wanted to focus on trying to pay attention in each class and doing each subject's assignments during the afternoon's Study Hall. Not easy with all the noise and disruptions. At every lunchtime when all the kids were present, Joe constantly heard about the travails of the upper classmates. It was like the daily gossip round the lunch tables. 'Who just got pregnant, who was just arrested for armed burglary, who was just released for unarmed robbery, who was caught carrying a gun into school, what little girl was accidently shot this past weekend a block from school, which store might be the next mass shoplifting target, which street corner had the cheapest crack cocaine, who was selling marijuana cigarettes in school this week, which stupid kid had a parent trying to get them transferred to a charter school, which kids did not show up at the start of this school year because they got scholarships into private schools because they were considered from "low income families with inequities in education," which graduating kids got college scholarships for their athletic abilities, especially in basketball and football, who did not return to school this year because they decided to drop out, where can a kid get a part time or full time job'. Joe heard it all and decided he wanted to tell Mama Sarah not only all of this, but also about his good opportunity, or would it be a bad decision, to become a shoplifter. He already knew the answer.

Joe learned by the end of the week that buddy Charles had also gotten himself involved in the shoplifting business. "Joe, it's only what they call a misdemeanor in the law. That ain't considered anything serious or involves jailtime like a big armed robbery they call a felony. I can tell you where the Mexicans meet this weekend. I wasn't in on the big deal last weekend like you were, but it's better to operate on your own. It's easy money. Come on, bro. What say you? You and me a team."

"Yes, yes, bro, I am seriously thinking about it. Where is the location? Probably see you there." Joe responded quickly and forcefully to his friend but underneath this false expression, his feelings were quite clear. He had already hesitated with his brother to avoid his anger or disappointment. And he had spilled the beans to Mama Sarah. About the choice. He was not going to be a shoplifter but had left the decision open to friend Charles, brother William, and to beloved Mama

Sarah. He had felt he did not want to disappoint those closest to him, but he also had to feel resolve.

Late Saturday afternoon, after Joe had returned from the basketball court, Ella announced to Etta and Joe that she was going out with friends and that she had it setup for them to join Beatrice and Sarah for dinner next door. All during the ensuing dinner Joe quietly wrestled with the thought of how he would approach his wise old great grandmother with his dilemma, or should he not bother her with it and let his own decision stay quiet. But as the table cleared, he found he had no choice. He had to tell her everything.

"Hey my boy, let them do the dishes. Let's talk. Want to know what is going on in my boy's new life in high school." Joe nodded and politely responded "Thank you for having me for a terrific dinner." He thought about her speaking in perfect English to him and he now responding in turn. He laughed to himself as he would continue to speak to his friend Charles in their familiar street talk.

On the living room couch together, Mama started the conversation simply: "So Joe, you tell me, how is it going?" She then smiled and laughed "Any conflicts?"

Joe sat back and grinned. This woman is neat, so disarming, so calm, so relaxing for me. Compared to weeks ago where he just basically listened to her, sometimes understanding sometimes not, he now felt he was up to speed. He had absorbed so much of what she had preached to him, his moral guide, that these early school days seemed like a century of experience for him, and that he could talk about anything with her. "Yes, lots of conflicts. Many things Mama. You were right, high school has lots of chaotic moments, many kids really good, some really bad. Lots of disruptions. My friend Charles in trouble, loosing his cool and fighting in the cafeteria. I have a great history teacher I'll tell you about, but what is really on my mind is something else. You have told me to think before acting. Well, I didn't last Saturday night, but I don't think I was identified so I don't think I'm in trouble." He paused.

"Go on, Joe. I'm listening," Sarah said calmly.

"Well, William talked me into a shoplifting raid on a CVS store last Saturday night, and I did the whole thing, including getting twenty dollars for what I stole." He paused again.

"Yes, I saw the whole thing on TV, local news. You must know all those stores have cameras everywhere. Go on."

Joe gulped and had the quick thought that he had now embarrassed himself in front of the one person in his life he loved the most, that he had disappointed her. She that had termed him "a good boy." But he knew deep down this is the one person he could talk to, the one person who might help him find his way in life. Then the conflicting thought 'who cares, whatever comes just comes, just ride along with whatever'.

Sarah sensed the confusion evident from Joe's facial expressions now. "Joe, I'm only here to express to you my learnings in life, to express my desires and wishes for you if they can be of benefit to you, but you are a young man now. You are going to make your own decisions. I no longer can tell you what to do, except I have been quite firm as to how you should respect the girls. But I am not your military commander. I can give you advice from a lifetime of experiences. I can tell you it's wiser to be on the honest side long term, that short term it may seem, well maybe smart, to take the dark side for your more immediate advantage. I pray you will know right from wrong, lawful from unlawful. I pray you know shoplifting is breaking the law, hurting someone else who paid to put those goods in the store, but it's easy to do and rewarding to you with little possible consequence, and to tell you that once you are in that frame of mind, you very well might be tempted to go on to bigger things with bigger potential returns but also bigger potential penalties if you get caught, like jailtime and loss of bigger, brighter opportunities." She became silent and stared straight ahead, obviously wanting Joe to say something. To make his own decision.

After a minute of the two in silence, only the distant arguing chatter of Beatrice and Etta in the kitchen, Joe spoke up. A seeming miracle to Sarah as young Joe's voice was clear and strong. "Mama, you told me the world is full of conflicts, big and small, sometimes violent, but that the world is also full of opportunities, personal opportunities if one only tries. I love my family, each and every one, but I know we can do better. I do want to be good. I want to be strong. I don't want to hurt anyone else. I do want to succeed, to achieve something good, to be like my history teacher and try to help others succeed. No, Mama, I am not going to shoplift, and I am going to put that twenty-dollar bill away, never spend it but keep it as a reminder that I did not earn it. It is not mine." There was a pause in the conversation. Mama Sarah looked straight ahead at the floor but beamed a smile in obvious delight, expressing the look of happiness in the face of this quite old, but very wise, lady. Her best mission in her remaining life – Joe. She reminisced about how good a job she had done raising her two boys, both outstanding in their long careers, but how she missed with daughter Beatrice, now matter how hard she tried to guide her. Some individuals can just be so different in their makeup, how they think and react to things, how they accept or reject advice, suggestions, and even commands. How remarkable now to hear this 14-year-old boy come out with such a strong statement about rejecting something that is so prevalent among his friends and schoolmates. Maybe I am blessed again she thought.

# 9

The next several weeks passed finding Joe in the same environment. The lunchroom talks about the next mass shoplifting event, all the kids with their individual stealing successes, the latest drug combinations and setting up for the next weekend parties with drugs and sex, the constant disruptions in the classrooms, except for one. Mr. Washington with his strong, standing, physical presence in front of his desk and his booming voice kept everyone in line. The kids were actually paying attention and learning some history of the world, especially the Black kids and their African heritage. Mama Sarah had informed Joe of a startling statistic: only 34% of Philadelphia school students were proficient in English and only 15% in math. She told him that if these numbers she had read about also included private and charter schools, then the public schools must really be bad and have lower scores. Over 30% of the kids never earn their high school diploma, nearly 40% in the big public schools, even though so many are given passing grades they never earned. To herself, she thought that maybe she should look into how to help Joe get into a charter school next year or even how to get selected for a scholarship to a private school. On the other hand, Joe had brought home his first report card – an A in every single subject. Public, charter, or private? A dilemma. But maybe, perhaps, Joe can stay where he is and somehow be a shining light for others to follow. What a great thought, she mused.

—⟐—

Joe was still going through a growth spurt. His shoe size was suddenly 10, his arm and chest muscles were clearly showing. At the start of the freshman basketball team tryouts in early November, he was 5 foot 10 inches tall and 150 pounds. He was dominant. The coach was delighted to welcome Joe and saw him destined to be the number one player on the team even though some kids were taller. Joe's playground exploits in the heat of the summer – passing, dribbling, running full speed, playing with the adept big kid – combined with his daily exercise routine, had put Joe into a commanding position. Now he just had to work on his shooting skills.

While Joe knew his outstanding first high school report card and his ease in making the freshman basketball team would please his mother and great grandmother, he still had some second thoughts. William treated the news of all A's with indifference, as did Etta. Perhaps brother and sister resented the stellar performance of their younger brother, he thought. Maybe I was supposed to be like them, destined to be an underperformer, a future high school dropout, a failure. There were other concerns as well. Charles let Joe know that things were really bad at home. Tony had finally paid Eddie the $500, but shortly after there had been a street corner drive by shooting with one bullet grazing Tony's head. Treated at the hospital and sent home, Tony nevertheless felt weak and distraught and constantly complained of headaches. Charles said their father would come home every couple of nights around 10 o'clock and just yell at his mother and at Tony. He kept demanding Tony do something about it, but easy to see that Tony wasn't physically up to it.

"Charles, Charles, listen bro. You alone can not fix this. Do not do anything foolish. I see you staring at Eddie in the hallways and lunchroom. He got paid by your brother. You do not know if he was in on the shooting. Stay cool, bro."

Later that day, the two were sitting together in the lunchroom when Joe noticed Charles had stopped eating and was just staring across the room at the older kids. His eyes were fixed on Eddie. Joe applied his reasoning to the emotions he thought must be swelling in Charles brain. I can't let him do this again, he thought. I'll try to play peacemaker. He rose and quickly walked towards Eddie's table thinking how he would handle this – calmly, non-threatening.

"Hey Eddie, hey what' up? Remember me, I'm your friend Tony's little brother's friend, Joe Robinson." Eddie stopped chatting with the kids next to and across from him and gave Joe a surprised look up. Joe kept talking without hesitation. "Yeah, ya probably heard Tony got a shot wound on his head last Saturday night. Wanted ya to know he's gonna be all right. His family little upset, but ya know I'm tellin' his little brother here, the one you gave a nice punch in the nose to here, that you got nothin' to do with no shootin' cause you got your money from Tony, right?"

Eddie at first continued his blank look up at Joe who was wearing a tight tee shirt exposing his newly formed muscles and who had spoken in a commanding tone, just like Mr. Washington. "No man, no way, I don't do no shootin' stuff. You tell them I'm cool, man." Joe gave Eddie a quick nod, a thumbs up. Joe returned back to the table to see an irritable Charles about to get up.

"Sit, Charles sit. Let's finish our lunch. All's okay. He has nothing to do with your brother's shooting." Calm pursued. That evening, Joe could not wait to tell Mama all about what had happened that day with Charles and Eddie. She put her hand on his knee and tapped it lightly as she turned and extended a warm smile.

"Joe, my boy, you are a learning dear. Your first experience in the art of conflict resolution without resorting to violence."

〰〰

"Without resorting to violence." Joe could not get that thought out of his head. *Confusing, confusing,* he kept thinking. *But I put myself in the middle and got both sides calmed down.*

The following Friday night, he turned down Charles' request to go to a party to be hosted by one of the 9th grade girls in their class. Apparently, her parents were going to be away, and it sounded to Charles like a great time for a group to get together, and who knows to do what. But Joe just had to pursue things with wise old Mama Sarah. He knew that William had purchased her a nice TV and a personal laptop computer.

After dinner with Mom and Etta, Joe went over, knocked, and then using his key went into Mama's house. MomMom Beatrice was dozing on the couch while Sarah was intently watching TV. "Mama, can I sit in with you?" He pulled over an adjoining chair while she instantly gave him a warm smile and put the TV on mute.

"My handsome young man. Sure you can. You're home on a Friday night?"

"Yes, Mama. Not much going on tonight."

Sarah's first thought was *wow, my teaching has paid off. His English is perfect. But I wonder what's up?*

"Mama, something you have said many times. Now Mr. Washington is using it to describe all the wars taken place over the centuries. It's what I have seen on the playground basketball court, on the school playground, in the lunchroom, with William telling me about his gang, the talk around the older kids. Violence, Mama, violence. What's going on? Can we really resolve it?" He hesitated, looked down at the floor, and then up at her.

"You mean beyond what you just did in the lunchroom?" Sarah reached for the TV changer on her lap and turned the TV off, then opened her laptop computer sitting on a table next to her and placed it on her lap. "Okay, listen up. I can replay the six o'clock local news. You will see, three shot on a corner in North Philadelphia last night, one dead at scene, one died going to hospital, one in critical condition at the hospital. No suspects caught yesterday. Funeral services for a 6-year-old girl killed in a drive by shooting last Saturday night. No suspects yet. Police car turned over and set on fire; two officers in hospital. One suspect in custody. Same stories across the country. Overseas, eleven civilians killed in drone attack on eastern city in Ukraine, hundreds of Russian soldiers killed in cluster bomb retaliation, climbing death toll in an African nation government rebellion, Israel in a war with Palestinian terrorists.... Then there are the natural deaths, floods, fires, tornados.... Then Joe there are the entertainment deaths we talked about before, movies, games. Then there is the sporting violence short of death – fighting matches, even with the girls on tv with skimpy gloves on punching and kicking, ice hockey fights and so on and so on.... You are asking me, Joe, what's all this violence stuff?" She paused and glanced at Joe's reaction so far. He simply nodded begging her to go on. "We covered that before so what are you asking me? We have talked about man born to be disorderly, right? So, I told you why we have religions, rules, customs, laws. Most of us can be very orderly and worthy of good things when we are raised or exposed to some solid structure in our lives, or to the values of discipline and self-discipline. We covered that, right?" Joe nodded again. "Okay, my boy, let's face reality. No one living today is going to get rid of this violence we see among certain leaders in certain nations. We thought it might be over after World War II, but then we had Korea, Vietnam, 911, Iraq, Afghanistan, Ukraine, Israel. Countries all over the world building up weapons of war, like our own concerns about North Korea, Iran, Russia, China. Joe, for quite a while now looking ahead, you and I are not going to solve that dreary outlook. Neither, young man, are you and I going to do much about violence as an entertainment attraction. Or the occasional violence committed by a brain damaged person who suddenly believes in his sick mind that he has to take certain people out.... But Joe, but you young man, can think about the violence around you and how it impacts your education and your neighborhood. About the violence among school kids, young adults, in our so called 'less privileged neighborhoods', much related to too many drugs and guns. And the problem of reducing our police forces or not prosecuting those who break our laws. The experience so far showing those moves reduce the consequences of doing wrong resulting in more violence not less. More lenience results in more rule breaking. Yes, my boy, disorderly man. It starts with constant **conflicts** our way of life.

"Think I'm understanding you Mama, but what the heck can I do? Are you saying with all this conflict and violence around us, what you have taught me and now I see it, disorderly people not agreeing on this and that, selfishness, personal power, personal profit, revenge, greedy, gaining an advantage, all this stuff … that I can do anything about it? Just live with it?"

Mama Sarah turned her head from the screens and looked right into Joe's eyes. "Yes," she replied in a firm tone of voice. "You can. In your school, in your neighborhood. Maybe for all of Philadelphia, maybe for all of our inner cities. But at least, just be a Philadelphian." Joe looked at her bewildered, beginning if for the first time thinking his older, wiser, and learned great grandmother had just lost her mind. Given up. Crazily thinking that 14 year old Joe Robinson had any destiny in this resolving this madness.

—⚉—

Other than his time on the playground basketball court that weekend, Joe felt he couldn't wait to get to school Monday. He kept thinking about what Mama Sarah had told him Friday after dinner. We are helpless in eliminating violence in all walks of life, but maybe, just maybe, something can be done about it in our inner cities, in our so called "poor" neighborhoods. Mr. Washington, so commanding in his classroom, so knowledgeable about the history of mankind, *I can't wait to talk to him.*

When the bell went off ending Monday's History class, Joe scurried to the front of the classroom and put his face right up to Mr. Washington's. "Mr. Washington, can I talk to you after school today? I need your views on something important." The usual stern look on Joe's teacher's face turned to one of pleasant surprise, then to one of feeling important.

"Why sure, Joe Robinson. You are my best student. I will be glad to meet with you. Right back in this classroom, say at three o'clock." While Joe nodded and maintained his serious look, Mr. Washington gave way to a slight smile, the first that Joe had witnessed from this learned man. Joe quickly moved on to his next morning class, but promptly at three p.m. was back there again just before Mr. Washington appeared a moment later. "So, young man, what's up? Sit down here. What do you want to talk about?" As Joe sat down as directed in a front row desk, he at first sensed a feeling of intimidation as this distinguished looking middle-aged man sat down next to him in the adjoining desk chair. Was he going to be at a loss for words? He was not accustomed to speaking to grown up men before let alone someone he so admired.

Quietly but firmly, he began. "Yes, Mr. Washington, I have a great grandmother, the only one in our family who went to college. She is very smart. My great grandfather died before I was born. I don't have a grandfather, and I don't know who my father is…." He paused.

Mr. Washington sensed the discomfort and immediately interrupted. "Oh, right, perfectly normal for us stuck in this part of our great city," and he let out a gentle laugh as he looked squarely into Joe's eyes maintaining his warm smile. "Go on, go."

Joe took a deep breath and could feel his tense shoulders relax. "Well, okay, yes … so she has been talking to me about the issue of conflict and violence, how no two people always think alike, how they can disagree so much, how so many of us are born disorderly, how conflict is a normal part of our human nature and that's why it's so common."

"And she has taught you right, as I am teaching you in my class. That's why our human history has been one of never-ending wars. Right? Go on, go on."

Joe responded, "Yes, wars among tribes, societies, nations, like in our history book, but wars also among gangs, like right here today in our streets." Mr. Washington's facial expression changed dramatically, now turning serious. He thought, what is this kid driving at?

"Okay, right, son. But what can I do for you?"

"Is all this violent kind of conflict because we now have

drugs and guns in our neighborhoods? I was told we didn't have all this years ago. How can we get educated today? All my classes except yours are disruptive. How do you do it?" The conversation paused.

Mr. Washington squirmed in the desk chair, one slightly too small for his large mature frame. "Joe, let me try to give you a different kind of history. We are a nation of immigrants. Our city here always had neighborhoods, areas of different heritages – early on the English, the Dutch, the Swedes, the Germans, then the Jews, Italians, Irish, then the Black Africans and Hispanics. Today, from around the world. Of course, there were always conflicts, like your great grandmother says, but we had strong churches, mild movies, strong police forces keeping conflicts from getting too far out of hand, and yes like you said, we didn't have the drug and gun culture we have today while at the same time we have less of a police force and less criminal prosecution, But let me tell you, there was always a problem of neighborhood schools. When I was about to enter high school, my father had me see an old movie, from way back 1955, *Blackboard Jungle*, where the classroom kids were portrayed as illiterate, criminal, hoodlums, thugs, a few accused of attempted rape and armed robbery. Sure, that was in a small neighborhood in New York, but the point is we had the same poor education here in Philadelphia and on to today in certain neighborhoods, including this one. Today, Joe, much of this is a problem for Black people like you and me. Discrimination against the Irish and Italians is pretty much gone, and legally discrimination against Blacks disappeared way back in 1965 with the Civil Rights and Voting laws. You know we have Black mayors now, Black police chiefs, broadcasters on TV, a former Black president, and so on, but so many of us still live in the poor parts of our cities, have disadvantages in housing, jobs, education. Some of us today, the so called 'underprivileged', are getting special treatment, all in the name of creating the so-called diversity, equity and inclusion movement. I am all for that as long as individual merit is also included.... And you asked how do I maintain a learning environment in a public school marred by rudeness, disorderliness." Joe sat up more attentive than ever. "Well, son, teachers are taught to impart their subject matter, not to be a policemen. We belong to strong unions that have fought and won for us good wages, lots of time off, and nice pensions when we retire. Many teachers hang around for those benefits even though their classrooms are somewhat chaotic, and their school neighborhoods can be unsafe. Me? I love history. I try to convey a message that history is where we all came from and a clue as to where we are going. I try to make it personal. I try at the start to show that I care about you kids. I stand up in front of my desk. I try to speak firmly. From the outset, I want to convey the appearance in all this of structure, of discipline. There is the story that fathers provide structure and discipline, and I think you know from your own experience that three fourths of the black babies born in Philadelphia do not have a father at home. So where can the structure and discipline come from to raise a kid who will stay honest and complete his or her schooling? The truth is Joe that even with a father at home, that father has to be honest and disciplined himself, and sometimes I wonder about that." Another pause while Joe sat attentive but silent. "So my boy, was that helpful? Lots more guns and drugs today, but still poor education. Is it ongoing discrimination against us? Or is it the fault of our own Black culture? You think I really know? Well, I'll tell you. I think history will be on our side when we get the right leaders. And you, you gonna solve all this?"

Joe looked at his teacher square in the eye. He had no idea that he could now sound so resolved at his young age as he spoke to his teacher: "Mr. Washington, I know I am only fourteen years old, but I believe I have made a decision. I just hope my brother, my sister, my friends, this school, all this, won't change me for the worst…. I want to be like you, like my great grandmother, Mama Sarah, and even more. I want to not just understand. But more, I want to influence kids, people, my neighborhood. She thinks if I am an A student and good at basketball, maybe I can be pulled out, an underprivileged from poverty, and get an 'equity' scholarship at a private school, but I told her I want to stay here. I want to see discipline. I want to make a difference. I've seen that slogan. I…." Joe paused, dropping his head down, not knowing what more he could say. Ron Washington reached his arm out towards Joe, patting his student approvingly on the boy's shoulder, a sense of pride overcoming him. Quite a day, they both thought to themselves.

# 10

The routine of after school classes right to basketball practice, five days a week, started out great for Joe. The freshman coach, Sonny Smith, the young energetic Mr. Smith, had never extended his playing days beyond his high school basketball experience. His team was with a high school located in the rough neighborhoods of Baltimore, Maryland. His mother had persuaded him to finish high school, play basketball, and earn a college degree at a historically black college. She was thrilled that he had now landed this job teaching gym class and coaching freshman basketball at this high school in Philadelphia. The pay was good, the benefits great, and to her he seemed quite happy each time he returned home for a holiday break. What she did not know was that he had kept his overly tough demeanor ongoing as a coach, that he clearly let these young boys know that **his** manner of discipline was supreme.

"Robinson, we have a scrimmage comin' up tomorrow right here with a weak team before our first game next Wednesday. You are my number one player. You got good moves. Strong. I'm namin' you Captain. You listen to me each time out. Got it, boy? And you call me 'sir' not 'coach'." Joe looked at him speechless but nodded as though he understood. He felt good inside about the praise but could not comprehend his new coach's bravado.

The visiting team warming up the next afternoon looked like they had a few tall kids, but they were pretty skinny looking. As the practice game started, Joe noted his opponents seemed sluggish, not one was very adept moving the ball around or shooting. Nevertheless, Mr. Smith never shut up from his standing position on the sidelines. Five minutes into the scrimmage, the coach yelled at Joe to call time out. The score, not kept on the electrical scoreboard, must have been something like 12 to 2, with Joe scoring six of his team's points. He was now learning to shoot, far beyond his playground experience.

"Jesus! You guys are letting them shoot. Ther're no damn good, but next week we play a real team," coach Smith hollered. "Robinson! You get in their face, block them with your hips, push your fists into their stomach as they shoot the ball. The damn refs next week won't even see it if you do it right. Joe knew exactly what Mr. Smith meant. That was standard playground ball, but Joe thought school basketball would be more legitimate. He had watched many college and pro games on TV with Mama Sarah, and when players were fouled shooting the ball the referees blew their whistles and called the offenses.

—◊—

It seemed to Joe that it was no time before the first real game of the season. The visiting team was Overbrook from West Philadelphia. Joe gave a long glance at them during the warmup drills. They appeared so much bigger than his own teammates. He reviewed in his mind the style he knew Coach Smith wanted him to play. Left hand up in the face of the shooter, right hand digging into his opponent's stomach just below his ribs, a classic move from his playground days. Done right, the ref will never see it. Joe's whole team was drilled this way and ready.

"Robinson, I have a report. You guardin' their best shooter, Carter is his name. I'll find out which one and tell you. He's six feet two, bout four inches taller than you, but you stick right on him, got it? Hands boys, active hands." Joe nodded trying to display some confidence, but those guys at the end sure seemed much bigger and stronger looking than his squad. This was Joe's first official game with real referees, two of them. And it was not more than two minutes into the game when Joe was called twice to give up the ball, once for walking and the second for palming. Joe felt confused as not only was his style typical playground ball handling, but watching the pros play on TV, walking and palming were so much more evident and common than anything he had just done. "Christ, Robinson!" He could hear Coach Smith yell from the sidelines. "You're not on the playground. Handle the damn ball."

Joe felt dazed for a moment, but then he drove in for a shot running full speed to the right of the basket and it poured in. His first basket on his high school's floor. He felt renewed. The game proceeded with Joe handling the ball more carefully, his speed and dribbling far exceeding any other player on the floor. His defense against Carter was perfect. One hand waving innocently in front of Carter's face, the other by disguise digging into Carter's stomach. Carter complained several times to the referee but to no avail. Half a dozen times he yelled at Joe, "Stop that shit, man. This ain't no damn playground ball." Joe pretended he didn't hear. When the final horn blew, Joe's team was up 48 to 40, with Joe scoring 24 points, half his team's total, but it was not over. While a jubilant Coach Smith headed to the locker room with his joyous team following behind him, Joe heard his name called out twice from someone on the visiting team, now gathered together and headed towards the exit door. Joe paused mid court as two of Overbrook's bigger players approached him with Carter right behind. It happened so fast. He heard from one of them: "Nice game Robinson." And in a flash the two bigger players grabbed Joe by his two arms while Carter took dead aim and unleashed a fist right into Joe's nose. Dazed and feeling the sharp pain as he half fell holding his nose, Joe could hear "Told ya man, this ain't no playground ball." The three adversaries quickly turned towards their waiting teammates, and they all ran together to the exit door. Down on one knee, Joe felt the blood rushing out his nose, the pain barely subsiding.

—⁘—

That evening's chat with Mama Sarah was difficult. At dinner, William, Etta, Grandmom Beatrice had all heard Joe's tale of how he had incurred such a swollen nose. His tone was quiet, no emotion, just the story of the events. Now, later with Mama, he was not sure how to begin…. She broke the ice. "Joe, know you must be confused. You know exactly from all our talks how and why these things happen. Think you are puzzled what you can possibly do about it now that this disorderliness, this constant conflict is directly affecting you. Let's try to think this through. What happens in conflict? The smarter guy prevails. The stronger guy prevails. The more devious guy prevails. The better armed guy prevails. The one with more powerful resources prevails. Advances among the ones more civilized, why they invent games, like sports, where injury can occur but not to the death, and scores and rules are introduced to keep the conflict orderly even to the point of fun. For the first time, you were introduced to that more civilized element, sports, and yet rules were first broken without correction, without punishment, until the end of the game. Well maybe in that kid Carter's point of view, justice was eventually served because you broke the rules against him first. The conflict mediator, the ref, didn't see the conflict. So, you eventually got punished in the most basic way because you violated him the whole game. That's one way of him settling the score. He landed a good punch right into your face. At least he didn't shoot you." She tried to have him glance at a slight smile with that comment.

"So unresolved conflicts, with no one in the middle, can't be settled without violence in some form or other, always a winner and a loser? Is that what you are saying, Mama? That's what you are saying?"

"Your perfect English, my boy, your perfect English. Good!"

"Who cares about that. What good does that do me?"

"The good that it does you, dear Joe, is that it allows you to sit here and talk with me. That's what. And maybe someday ahead, you will see, you will see a way ahead. Maybe conflicts can be settled fairly."

"I don't know Mama, I don't know," Joe replied meekly.

"Well, as we spoke before, you can always consider getting away from this mess. I just read that more money is going towards parents' choice in schools, you know charter schools, and you are already an honor student and a basketball star so you might even qualify for a scholarship at a private school. Sound good?" Mama Sarah spoke these words softly, solemnly, as though maybe she wasn't meaning what she was saying. But her smile broke through as she listened to Joe's reply.

"Mama! We discussed this before. No, I'm staying here. All that so called goodness, correcting the inequity you were talking about; no, that all is a lot of good work that is benefiting some, a minority of kids, but the majority around here, still left behind. Who stops the kid putting his fist into the shooter's stomach so the ref can't see it, who stops the kid fouled from punching the other kid out, who stops the noise in the classroom, the disrespect towards the teachers, the turmoil in the lunchroom, the selling of drugs in school, in the playground, on the street corners, who gets the father to come forward and help take care of the kid? Not just who, Mama, but how?

"You are right, son. No leader we have now, and certainly none of the politicians we've had so far. Way back when I was in college, I learned conflict resolution programs were commonly offered in our colleges, in the larger companies, in government. That was all easy because your job was at stake. You cooperated. In government, we have parties that rule by majority vote. Democracy. How does it work? It works by the conflicting persons with a moderator present allowing both sides to express what they want, then finding some common grounds they can agree on as well as partially giving up something. That's called the art of compromise. It's how our nation was founded. All men created equal, no king, except for us blacks left out so that the big southern state of Virginia would stay in. The 1776 Declaration of Independence. Then eleven years later, our Constitution, nothing accomplished in the heat of the summer until our great Philadelphian Ben Franklin forced the compromise. Those who wanted a strong federal government gave a little. Those who wanted thirteen nations or strong states under a weak federal government gave a little. They reached a compromise. Joe, that's why the little states as well as the big states each get two senators and why the House of Representatives get representatives based on their state's population. And hey, I hear even your school district has counselors who will help out in trying to compromise conflict situations, but of course it's limited in scope and influence…." A pause while Joe maintained a stare down to the floor and Mama took a deep breath.

Joe finally regained his pitch. "But my history teacher said no one compromised when Russian tanks drove into Ukraine unwanted and uninvited. And he said no one is compromising about our country having a strong military when Russia, China, North Korea, Iran threaten our democracy. And no one compromised when my coach orders me to do one thing and the best player on the other team doesn't put up with it. Easy word Mama but not out here in this neighborhood. And hey, my coach is not going to back off when his method worked against a bigger team. I was just lucky when I got my friend Charles to back off because his brother Tony did pay off his debt to Eddie."

Mama replied, "So civilization means setting rules and everyone abides by them so that things are orderly. Those who break the rules are punished. That creates discipline. Forced discipline creates self-discipline. Society, individuals, thrive, advance, achieve. For the most part, that is America, Joe. Even so, we have some who have a tarnish from their raising, some are overly greedy, some are mentally imbalanced. No such thing as perfection. Never will be. Problem here is that so many of our neighborhoods don't live up to that standard of discipline. We are told we are in poverty, underprivileged, been kept back as victims of long-ago slavery. Discriminated against as victims of white supremacy. I hear all this on TV Joe. I cannot tell you how much is true, but I do know we living here have not made much progress the last 75 years. Our great Martin Luther King did so much back then to lead us out of discrimination. The Voting Rights Act allowed us today to have black governors, mayors, police chiefs. But still, I learned that only nine percent of us have higher incomes than the median white income. Certainly Black sports stars, entertainers. So many of us are making it today...but we still have the back streets of Philadelphia, Chicago, Baltimore and many more. So, Joe, Joe, what to do, we ...." Joe was listening intently. Mama's psychology was working, forcing Joe to think.

It was getting late, but suddenly Joe had a new look on his face. Eyes straight ahead, jaw set. Fourteen years old – an ardent warlord, or a skilled compromiser? Did not matter which right now he might become. On his face was a new look of determination.

# 11

Two days later at Thursday's basketball practice, Joe came up with an idea. On Wednesday, the day after the team's victory over Overbrook, Coach Smith was completely ignoring Joe's swollen nose while Joe's teammates were having a good laugh. They too were using the two hands defensive move their coach had demanded of them but only sparingly and weakly as they were all guarding the weaker players, and Coach Smith was not watching them as closely as he had his eyes on his offensive/defensive star Joe Robinson.

"Coach, I have a great idea. No problem the bloody nose, but if the next guy punches me in the eye, I may not be able to see for the next game. I'll be no good to you. I think I have a defensive move to stop the shooters but not committing a foul. Nobody gets pissed off." Joe put his face right in front, up close to Coach Smith's so that the coach could not miss the swollen nose.

"What you talkin' bout, boy? I'm the coach, not you." He obviously looked disturbed and wanted to show this kid that he was in charge, but he could not miss the swollen nose and even wondered if it was broken.

Joe did not back down. "Coach, if we make an extra effort

to really get our hands up in the shooters' faces and let out a "defense" cry before the ball is released, the shooter will be bothered. The refs won't even hear it, but still, it's legitimate. We use this on the playground a lot and it works."

Coach Smith backed up, and as he was turning away said aloud "Go practice shooting your foul shots, Robinson."

At 2:15 on Friday afternoon, the school bus was parked outside awaiting the ten members of the freshman basketball team. The players were already dressed for the game as they boarded the bus. The drive was less than a half hour up to Northeast High School for the 3:30 start. Coach Smith signaled for quiet after departure. "Okay, team listen up. Same starting team as Tuesday. All out hustle, bust your asses and everyone will play, hard! One change, instead of hiding your left hand from the refs and digging into the stomach of the shooter with your left fist, get both hands up high and yell "defense" into the shooter's face. Disturb his rhythm. Got it?" Wow, impossible not to see the slight smile breaking out on Joe's face.

The Northeast players did not look as tall and strong as Overbrook's, but as the game progressed, it was obvious they were good ball handlers, good rebounders, and were making their open fast break shots. But in the close up play, Joe's new technique on guarding shots was working well. The

Northeast players were obviously bothered by the tight hands up defense and the sound in their ears as they attempted their shots. At halftime the score was 20-20, with Joe again scoring half of his team's points. Coach Smith was harsh as he raised his voice. "Playing hard means playing hard. We miss a shot and don't get the rebound, you knuckleheads hustle back to the other end as fast as you can. Interrupt their flow, stop their fast breaks. They have almost all their points on fast breaks. Do you guys know what I'm talkin' bout? I'm gonna keep substitutin' to keep fresh legs in there." Joe noticed almost the whole nine other guys on his team were nodding affirmative. Joe had the fleeting thought that this was what good coaching was all about. The second half was a runaway. Joe hustled and poured in the points. The defense was energetic and was decisive in stopping the Northeast fast break. Their aggressive hands up and disturbing sounds defense worked like a charm. Northeast only scored eight points in the third quarter and only six in the last, against wound-up Joe and his newly challenged teammates. Final score 55 to 34, with Joe accounting for 30 of his team's total.

The following day, at Saturday's playground games, the big kid was no longer there, tied up now as a star on the high school team. Young Joe Robinson was now the player of notice. A star is born.

—⁓—

Sunday evening's family dinner was at Sarah and Beatrice's home, but this time Mom Ella was the chief chef. Her preparation of a roast, baked potatoes, and string beans was perfect, a nice family setting. For a home in this untidy neighborhood, its furnishings were unusually up scale. That feature was through the generosity of William, but none of the ladies questioned him on where and how he earned the money to buy such nice curtains, chairs, lamps, dishes, and silverware, although they all knew. After dessert and before anyone could leave the table, the evening's tranquility was broken by Ella. Still sitting but looking sternly at her three children, she voiced her motherly sense of command. "Before you all get goin', let me tell you I'm concerned. Don't know where y'all were last night, but you gotta be careful, especially on Saturday nights. Stay out of trouble, ya hear me? Last night, there were three shootings on our block, one kid was killed. When I work late, I'm afraid to walk home alone, but I have to do it. Too many guns and too many crazy people out there. Ya hear me?" With her lips trembling, her face frowning, she abruptly rose, cleared her empty dish and moved briskly towards the kitchen. Sarah, Beatrice, William, Etta, and Joe all looked down in silence until Mama Sarah spoke up. "Okay, everyone help clear the table. Joe, I'll see you in the living room."

Fifteen minutes later, the two were beginning their "chat". "Joe, your mom is right. You have to be careful out there.

Listen, I know what happened at your school Friday. You were at your game, but I know you must know. At your school just outside. You have metal detectors at your door. So, what happens? Do these guys hide their guns right outside? Big argument. Two boys, one girl were shot, lucky no one died."

"Yes, I heard about that at the playground yesterday. Don't know them."

"No matter. I follow this stuff, young man. Numbers a lot higher in total, but just looking at students in Philadelphia. Have to update, but just the first three months of this year with students, 100 shot, 18 killed. Now hear about Chicago, the worst. First eight months of this year all ages, 1700 shootings, 425 dead. And we want to defund the police? Sure a few bad white cops shoot a black here and there, but the big numbers are blacks shooting blacks. What are we going to do about that, Joe?"

For a change, fourteen-year-old Joe did not hesitate a response. "For one of many steps, we have to upgrade our whole Black culture, Mama. As you have told me, we have to stop calling ourselves 'underserved, under privileged, victims of slavery'...."

"And just how are we going to do that, Joe? Look, in the military, in the private schools, in the homes with a firm father figure, you have this: good behavior is rewarded, bad behavior is punished. You have discipline, order, but with us here, bad behavior goes unpunished, so it continues, and good behavior is rarely rewarded. Graduate from one of our inner-city high schools, where do you go? Into a military career, into a college and stay for four years, into a good-paying city job, but that's not the majority."

"So, Mama, we have to create a reward/punishment system and we have to create jobs for kids coming out of school. No more handouts except for the handicapped."

"Great, Joe, great, but the politicians have been trying to create progress for us for the last 50 years, but what do we have?" Mama Sarah could feel delight welling up inside as she now could challenge her young great grandson, and he was coming up with positive thoughts. She continued, "Listen, there are more statistics I keep track of. I'll write this down for you, but you listen first. These are recent numbers for the big public high schools you will be playing basketball against…. Okay, so Philadelphia has over 200 district schools with 76 high schools, couple hundred thousand kids with 65,000 in charter schools, those schools graduating 86% from high school while our other public schools only graduate less than 70%. Your brother and sister, Joe…. Okay, so what I'm going to list in order is the percentage of Philadelphia public high school students who are considered by standardized testing to be proficient in English, then in Math, then who graduate, then who go to college, then who attend more than 90% of school days, and lastly the percent who are suspended from school for extremely bad behavior, but as we know Joe that punishment may seem meaningless to those kids.

"Okay, so Overbrook, proficient English 15%, proficient Math 3%, graduate 72%, college 19%, attendance 6%, suspended 15%. West Philly 13%, zero, 70%, 36%, 31%, 19%. Roxborough 24%, 1%, 71%, 26%, 10%, 27%. John Bartram 7%, zero, 73%, 26%, 19% 15%. Thomas Edison 12%, 2%, 55%, 17%, 9%, 16%. Frankford 34%, 15%, 75%, 48%, 38%, 7%. Lincoln 19%, 6%, 62%, 29%, 24%, 12%. Ben Franklin 7%, 1%, 61%, 17%, 12%, 10%. Kensington 16%, 3%, 62%, 14%, 14%, 3%. Martin Luther King 12% English, zero Math, 45% graduate, 15% to college, 15% good attendance, 10% suspended. Northeast 50%, 13%, 73%, 55%, 30%, 10%....

"So, young man, not so great, eh?"

Joe's eyes were wide open. It was hard to believe these numbers, especially such low scores in Math. "Yet Mama, so many do graduate, and some go on to college even with such low scores in English and Math. I wonder...."

"You wonder how teachers simply feel their students cannot repeat grade after grade and you wonder how those college bound students really do thereafter. Young man, you straight A student, you sure have a challenge in front of you if you think you are going to help turn this decades old problem around." Her sharp stare at him now turned soft, warm, loving, with a new sense of admiration for this bright young man. Yes, *challenge him, but do not discourage him* were her deepest thoughts.

Joe had a difficult time falling asleep that night, even after an extra effort into his situp/pushup routine. He felt a little bit lost. William was out as usual. He thought of William, and of his best friend Charles. Over and over he was thinking to himself: 'How do you create discipline where there is no fear of punishment for bad behavior, and how do you create rewards for good behavior without handing out free candy?' Brother William has no fear of any authority except whether he might get shot by a competing drug dealer or his throat slit if he disobeys his own boss, and friend Charles has no moral authority except his father's occasional appearance home to rant at his mother. And all these high school kids Mama just talked about: what incentives do they have to learn well and what to look forward to after high school?.... Pure physical fatigue finally put him to sleep.

# 12

The next six weeks went by quickly. Basketball practice was intense, the twice a week games were tough but rewarding. Joe's energy sparked his teammates to play hard and of course Coach Smith's constant yelling was impossible not to hear. Only if you played your heart out did his egging on seem less bothersome. By Christmas vacation time, the team's record was fourteen wins and no losses, with Joe by far the team's leading scorer. Joe kept thinking about when he would have another chance to speak privately with his best teacher, Mr. Washington, but basketball and getting his schoolwork done efficiently at afternoon study hall seemed all time consuming. But a new revelation did come to Joe as he thought about the success of his basketball team and about the success of his school record. Perhaps the effort put into sports can be rewarding, perhaps create a sense of dignity, create a sense of self-worth, and the penalty of having an unhappy, ranting coach if you do not try hard is a nice punishment. He had heard talk of reducing after school activities as a way of saving money for the schools, but that would seem contrary to what the kids really needed. He was now thinking that these activities are just what these city kids especially need – a sense of belonging, a sense of accomplishment – a reward for good behavior! He could not wait to try out these thoughts on his wise old Mama Sarah and the very wise Mr. Washington. At the same time, it did not diminish his sudden good feelings by looking at his second report card and rushing home to show his mom, grandmother and great grandmother – straight A's again. If they all simply smile, now that is a real reward for good effort.

---

At the close of history class, the last day before the school's Christmas vacation period, Joe on the spur of the moment approached Ron Washington and spoke up clearly and strongly: "Mister Washington, I have been so busy with schoolwork and basketball that I haven't had a chance to talk with you some more, but…."

"Well, no problem son," he cut in with a warm smile and an unusual soft tone to his strong voice. "I know all about your good grades and your exploits on the basketball court. But hey listen, I would be glad to meet you for breakfast or lunch anytime the next few days. I'm not going anywhere over the holidays."

Joe gulped and tried hard not to show the mix of surprise and joy on his face. "Yeah, I mean yes, that would be great."

It was the very next morning the two met for breakfast

at a nearby diner. Ron secured a window table where the two could talk without being disturbed. "So go ahead young man, tell me what's on your mind." The long-time history teacher was obviously delighted a student of his wanted to have a private conversation, an event mostly lacking at this school.

"Well, Mr. Washington, you know, I'm in the typical neighborhood home around here. No father around, a working mother who tries to convey a sense of discipline for me and my brother and my sister, but she can't seem to do that very well, or I guess even want to do too much of that. I am learning so much in your history class, and it looks like we, you know, mankind, we are making progress as history proceeds forward, but yet we Blacks look like, well, we seem to still have a long way to go.... I just wanted to ask you what's really going on about our progress, and like I told you before, I have learned so much from my college educated great grandmother. She is certainly my home's substitute for a firm father figure, but I also wanted to hear your thoughts on...."

After a long pause where Ron Washington tried to put together what was on this young man's mind, the teacher of world history began. "Okay, we Blacks, now remember Joe many hundreds of years back we were natives in Africa running around living off the land. Remember the more advanced whites, they called themselves the more civilized, came and thrived on our natural resources and even our free labor – slavery. Although slavery was present around the world, even in Africa, in America slavery was used in our South to farm the tobacco and cotton needed for the white man's living and for his wealth. As you know we were legally freed back in 1865, but it took another one hundred years before segregation was officially ended. During those years other minority groups in America were also discriminated against like the Jews, Italians and Irish, but it was much easier for them to eventually integrate and assimilate into American culture because they were all white in skin color. Our black skin color remained a strike against us, even though more recently so many college-educated blacks and black athletes and entertainers have assimilated into American society. So why are we still stuck here in these surroundings? Why are our inner city schools doing so poorly, why are so many Blacks shooting other Blacks, why is it that television ads show prosperous black families but out on the streets it's Blacks raiding stores, and stealing hundreds of thousands of dollars' worth of goods, or stealing cars, or leading the drug gangs, or leading the abortion numbers Well, many don't want to hear this, but just maybe it's the Black culture, long time customs and beliefs, although I don't want to believe this. My friend teaching first grade tells me her kids come to school unruly, aggressive, don't sit still, don't listen. She says no wonder the inner city black high school kids are so deficient in English and Math. They never got started. Maybe the family breakdown, the loss of strong religious teachings, the welfare from the politicians making things too easy, the lack of respect for the honest policeman ... maybe a lot of factors causing all this. Or maybe it's a carryover of a long history of job discrimination and housing discrimination that's still holding us back. Maybe it's all of this combined.

"But young man, cultures can change, they can assimilate. Yet, difficult for us because on one side we are told we are up against the old-time white supremacy, that we are victims, that the whites owe us, that as a nation we have to create equity for the Blacks, not advancement based on merit. On the other side where there is growing resentment, we are told we have to buckle up, take responsibility, work harder, strengthen the family unit. So, this mutual resentment, this difference in opinion, Joe, is not getting us anywhere. The so-called solution in education among some is called school choice – the parents sending their kids to the better schools. And the better schools do produce better results. But Joe that cannot be a universal answer – much too expensive and too impractical physically, and still way too many kids left behind. And how in the world do you convince fathers to be at home with their kids and enforce discipline or how in the world do you change the elementary school where kids now come to school now completely unruly and then get them to behave and learn?"

Joe was listening intently but had to interrupt. "But you

do it, Mr. Washington. Your class is calm. Everyone is paying attention. Why can't...."

"We discussed this before Joe. I am not changing one bit the failings of my kids in English and Math or their habits elsewhere. They are behaving in my class, and hopefully learning something worthwhile, only because as you remember from the first moment, I took command. I stood erect at the front of my desk and as you know I have a booming voice, and I let them know if they listen up they will learn where they came from and hopefully help them know where they are going. A voice of authority, a form of discipline, a display of a care for them. Unfortunately, as we just reviewed, most of we inner city blacks have gone nowhere the last 60 years. But I am delighted Joe to be here with you, young man.... Joe Robinson. You may be the exception."

Joe nodded in a look of appreciation from this learned man, but deep inside he was trying to balance a feeling of determination against a feeling of despair. What are the odds he thought to himself.

# 13

Compared to many families on Joe's block, Christmas was rather a fun, rewarding time. Perhaps because Mom Ella had a job earning some decent money, and because even MomMom Beatrice had occasional income from a part time cleaning job, and because of government welfare and government food stamps, but Christmas plenty came mostly because William had plenty of cash from his gang's drug dealing. Plenty of decorations, lots of presents.

"Joe, I know all your friends have these," Ella voiced out right after Christmas dinner. "I always insisted you were not ready, and I forbid it til now hopin' you would not get destroyed by Facebook, Tiktok, Instagram and all the rest of that garbage, but you do need it these days. Open it, son," and she handed him a small, gift-wrapped package. Joe eagerly opened his present with a slight grin on his face. He knew the contents already as he had been telling his mom that all his friends had cell phones for quite some time now. A thousand bucks! In reality though, with playground basketball consuming his full summer days and now being a conscientious student, Joe had always felt he did not need the time-consuming efforts like sister Etta chatting away and staring at her cell phone end on end.

At the end of Christmas dinner, William quickly left the table, and the three ladies were busy clearing the dishes to the kitchen. Joe sat still patting his full stomach, looking quite content after that fabulous dinner while sister Etta sat unusually still, not reaching for her phone as usual.

"So Joe, you're one of us now. Want me to teach you how to get on social media?" She showed a huge warm smile, and this appearance set Joe back as he was not used to this kind of conversation lately with his sixteen-year-old sister. In their early years, they were gleeful companions constantly playing and carrying on together. Their horseplay never went too far, however, as there was always Mama Sarah clearly laying down the rules of good behavior. Have fun, don't go overboard. Manners, respect for your elders. She was very clear in her commands.

"Well, dear sister, I appreciate your offer, but I don't have time for that stuff. I'll just use it to catch up with my friends and for emergency contact…. But look, Etta, I understand. Fine, you are not in school. You have lots of friends. You should stay in touch." Etta smiled warmly back at him. They had not conversed like this for some time. Joe sensed the opening. "Yes, listen, know it's not my business, sis, but our dear Mama Sarah and a certain teacher at school really have me thinking lately about a lot of things." He looked straight into her face to sense whether she was receptive to his new and surprising approach. She stared right back, nodded, and maintained her smile. "Okay, can I ask you this, sis? What is the most important issue, the main issue, that sixteen- year- old kids talk about, are concerned about? Is it their schoolwork, their acceptance with friends, is it staying away from or the opposite doing alcohol and drugs, or going to parties on weekends, or having a best friend, or boys appearing strong, tough, or girls appearing pretty, or ... I'm sorry, but girls appealing too much to boys loaded with male testosterone and getting pregnant." Joe knew that last one might have taken a step too far as young Etta was still having an ongoing debate with her mom and grandmom about having an abortion. Etta's smile was gone. She looked down but showed no sign of leaving the table.

"Young brother, yes, I know the chemistry. Boys starting at your age produce strong hormones that give them strength and sexual desires. They say that every fifteen-year boy has one wish in life—to get laid before he turns sixteen. But we girls also produce sex hormones, mostly for getting a healthy baby born, but also the desire to be hugged, loved, appreciated. Most of us though want to be careful, attract the boys but don't let them go all the way, at least not with full protection against getting pregnant. We want to be careful, but Joe, I messed up. I got drunk at a party. I was near passed out. Must have been five guys who gang raped me. I had no resistance. Not one of those guys will submit to a DNA test to see who the father is, and I cannot take them to court to force it because they all claim they were never at that party and have witness friends to back them. The other girls there don't know who did what. They were all drunk too.…. And also, all those other points you made about important issues – they are all true too. Lots of things on the minds of a sixteen-year-old kid. It all gets confusing." Etta put her head down, staring blankly towards the table's edge. Joe felt the tension, the emotion, but his blossoming maturity surprisingly spurred him on.

"Etta, I am so sorry. I don't want to be like that, like those guys at the party. I want to help you anyway I can. I'm here for you. If you have this kid of yours, I'll be here to help out." And then to hopefully see her regain her smile, he added "When I turn 15 this next year, I'm just going to smile at the girls and say "Come to our next game and see some really strong guys play good ball." Etta looked up at her younger brother, maybe, kind of, a warm look of admiration. Her smile returned.

—⁓—

The rest of Christmas vacation was not much fun for Joe. While the varsity basketball team was invited to participate in a holiday tournament, there were no games or practice times for the freshman team. The December weather was cool in Philadelphia, but not cold enough to diminish playground ball. Using his new cell phone, Joe seemed to be in constant touch with good friend Charles. They laughed easily together at the silliest things. Once they became teenagers, Charles' values were obviously lining up quite contrary to Joe's, but they were at ease with one another and could talk openly about any issue. The latest racket was Charles outlining in detail that raiding stores and selling the valuables was getting too risky as law enforcement was getting heat from city officials, store owners and the public while the racket of stealing cars could bring in more money and was easier without all the cameras in the stores identifying thieves. Although maybe impossible to do, Charles' older brother was trying to remove himself from his drug gang and move full time into stealing and selling cars. Joe just laughed at Charles' constant demands for the two of them to join up with Charles' brother. "Don't you see, bro, I am so busy here tryin' to clean up this playground with all the drug mess all over, fight off the bad guys on the court, and win a few games. Charles man, I just don't have no time, bro, to steal no cars." Joe wondered if he should bother taking the time to teach Charles good English. Fun to talk to Charles that way, but maybe too late for his friend to ever get it right.

But what he had said to Charles was right. The playground was a mess. Needles and trash on the ground, an 18-year-old kid, not a basketballer, getting shot in the stomach and luckily surviving after first responders got him to the hospital quickly, the police called in but getting no clues about the shooter. A kid 17 years old, also not a basketballer but a kid who just hung out there, getting knifed after the lights went out at 9 pm, pronounced dead at the hospital.

And then the basketball. Joe was glad the games at school had referees. Despite not calling many contact fouls, at least the paid refs kept the games from getting too far out of hand. Push and shove a little, but don't make it so obvious that a bunch of tough guys will punch you in the nose after the game.

At the playground, anything goes. The biggest, strongest, toughest guys rule. During the summer Joe was the little guy feeding the ball to the big kid. No one messed with him, so Joe survived well. Now without the big kid, Joe's determination to get faster and stronger was paying off. His twice to three a day routine of doing multiple sets of situps and pushups, while at the same time his body was going through a natural growth spurt, both meant the big kid backing him up was no longer needed. Not to say that was easy. Most of the games 14-year-old Joe played in were not with the 13 to16 year old kids. His quick speed, clever dribbling, and now with his new height and muscular strength, Joe played with the big boys, 18 and up. It was rough, pushing and shoving, occasional brawls with fists flying. No fouls were ever called, even a blow to the shooting arm let out only a "shit, man, get off my damn arm when I'm shootin.'"

Nevertheless, Joe relished these games during the holiday

break. Morning to night. Even when walking home, no lunch and asking the homebodies to tuck away his dinner, yes, headed home with some bruises and soreness and very hungry, he still felt good about himself. Sports he thought, even unregulated, made you tough. The kids getting knifed and shot were not the basketballers. The game was tough but not a killer. Joe thought long and hard about that.

# 14

The night before New Year's Eve found Joe wanting to get to bed early. It had been a long, hard day on the playground court, but after a huge, filling dinner that Mom had put away for him, he felt very tired but very content. Early to sleep he thought because Charles had convinced him to give up basketball the next day and plan to stay up late and party for New Year's Eve.

Before falling off to sleep, he was unexpectedly surprised when William entered their bedroom muttering away. "What's going on, Will?" Joe asked calmly, quietly.

"Shit, bro, this ain't workin' out. Go to sleep. You don't wanna know. Damn!"

"It's okay, William, you can talk to me. I'm not asleep yet. What's going on?"

"Shit, piss, God damn it. That bastard."

"Who are you talking about? Your gang leader?"

"Yeah, almost wanted to get you into this crap. Make some big money, but you went clean. Listnin' to Mama too much. She would be livin' just on food stamps and sleepin' on the couch downstairs if it wasn't for me.… But now, that bastard's cuttin' me back. I got just one corner now 'stead of four. Says he has a new kid better than me. Says I'm not aggressive enough. Give too much 'way to the tough guys. Give them too much discount."

"You can't talk to him? Tell him you can do better?"

"Shit, no. He's 30 years old, got five tough guys 'round him, all have guns. Not gonna be the next to get shot.... Damn, why you so different? That Mama got a spell over you? You don't don't even wanna do the shopliftin' stuff."

"William, come on. You know she is brilliant. She went to college, had a good job with the lawyers. She studied. She taught me we are all different. Our brains are all different. We are not going to think alike even if we are raised in the same house. What works for you may not work for me.... Listen, bro, I have decided I going to bend, but I am not going to break the law. I don't want to waste any time in jail or getting shot at. I'm doing real good in school, and I hope you come to one of my games. I'm not going to move over to a charter or private school even if they pay my way. No, I'm staying here, and I'm going to get a scholarship to a good college, not because I'm a Black from a poor area but because of my merits."

William's facial expression suddenly softened. What did he just hear? This is his little brother talking like this? Raised in the same house with no male figure around, just haggling women. Hard to digest, hard to understand. But so be it. Maybe I'll just have to start to admire him, and Mama

Sarah…. The gun he had pulled out of his dresser drawer and placed in his pants pocket after entering the room now went back into the drawer without Joe noticing any of his brother's movements.

Joe had just influenced someone in a positive way without his even realizing it.

—⁂—

Joe's new cell phone rang at 8 o'clock. The voice was an excited Charles. "Comin' over your house in ten minutes, bro. We'll walk to the party together." Joe had no details about this New Year's Eve party, only that this host girl named Theresa had said her parents were away and that she had the house to herself and her brother. Joe wondered why Charles wanted to start out so early, still four hours to go. Charles had only mentioned to be prepared to stay out very late.

"So, you're goin' to your first New Year's Eve party, huh son?" Joe's mother had said to Joe at the dinner table. The other three females just looked at him blankly, waiting for his response.

"Yes, Mom. All I know is it's at Theresa's house. She's in my class, but I have never talked with her. Guess it will be all ninth graders, maybe some of my friends from my basketball team, and of course Charles."

"She have any older brothers or sisters?" Ella pursued.

"Don't know that, maybe a brother."

"No matter, son. Look we here have all been through this. Comin' of age they call it. The girls are maturing, the boys are maturing. Sex, let's be polite and call it romance, is on everybody's minds. Often alcohol, or today marijuana, or God knows what else shows up. Things get loose. Young man, this is exactly how young girls get pregnant." Beatrice and Etta looked down, quiet. So did Joe. "Son, this is not a warning. Other than Mama, we got no saints at this table. As your mother, I just want you to be prepared. Wouldn't it be nice if no one got drunk and sick or passed out, if the girls are treated with respect and not violated, that the boys did not start a brawl, that nothing in Theresa's home got broken.... Have a good time, son."

Joe remained sheepishly silent as did the others. All finished up and cleaned up the dinner table together. A sobering moment in the young boy's growing up, but he accepted his mother's comments with seriousness.

—⟋⟍—

Turned out that Theresa only had one older brother, apparently one year out of high school and working in an undisclosed position at a nearby hospital. Before going out, he had done his younger sister a favor by filling the refrigerator with beer and by also filling a cooler on the floor with ice and quite a few wine bottles. Joe never noticed any drugs present, but he surely had learned from his playground experience the smell of marijuana. It was strong.

As the party proceeded, plenty of good hip-hop music blasting from the stereo setup, some cool dancing in the living room with all the chairs and tables pulled back as close to the walls as possible, and maybe about twenty kids there. Joe recognized just about everyone, all from his class at school. A couple of the boys he did not know seemed a bit older and acted a little more subdued, but always a beer in their hands.

Theresa was very, very pretty and caught Joe's eye immediately. He wondered why he never had paid her any attention at school. He felt the sudden sense of excitement in his chest when she approached him and asked him to dance with her. Joe had never danced with anyone before, but sure, he had watched enough TV with Mama Sarah to know what the moves are supposed to look like. For the first three hours of the party, the two had plenty of warm looks and friendly smiles towards each other, but with few words other than "thank you".

Quite accustomed to drinking beer at home, Charles was having a blast dancing with all the girls without the slightest hint that he was quickly getting looped but behaving. Not so with almost everyone else. Those first three hours were fun, fun, fun, but a half hour before striking midnight on the silenced TV, things had changed dramatically. These were mostly 14 year olds not used to drinking or smoking so much for so long. The boys were getting loud and foul mouthed, hanging on to the girls too closely; the girls showing signs they might have to run to the bathroom. When one boy threw up in the kitchen and two girls simultaneously in the living room, the party was doomed. Joe had noticed several of the boys and several of the girls were missing. Had they gone home early, or had they disappeared upstairs to the bedrooms? He remembered what his mother had said to him at dinner, but no matter, he simply reclined on the living room couch feeling a little stomach upset and a head that was feeling a little dizzy. Too much beer too fast? On the other hand, he could not take his eyes off Theresa, now seemingly somehow calmly trying to settle down the girls who had too much to drink or smoke. Was it her sense of responsibility for her parent's home or her caring for others or what? Joe wished silently to himself that he knew that answer. And then nothing.

"Joe, Joe, wake up. It's two o'clock. We gotta go home." Joe slowly opened his eyes, but he surely did not feel all that well. It was buddy Charles shaking his shoulders looking into his drowsy eyes. The room was silent, the music off. Except for the couch he had been reclining on, all the other furniture seemed back in place. The room was clean, no dirty ashtrays, empty beer or wine bottles. The air seemed to have a sense of smell of an air freshener generously sprayed about. Joe's glance finally turned away from Charles and the room décor to the person sitting right next to him. There was Theresa.

"Good morning, Joe. You missed a New Year's kiss, but I'm glad you rested with a good nap." That her voice and her smile were both so spectacular was all that speechless Joe could think about.

"You okay, bro? Can you talk? Can you get up?" Charles persisted, still standing right above the reclining Joe. "You know a lot of the stupid little kids here couldn't hold their booze, man, but this little lady here, wow who is she? She tossed those rascals upstairs right out of the house; she took care of the girls who threw up, even a couple of the guys; she cleaned up the spit up; she cleaned up the bottles and glasses; she straightened out the furniture; she made sure everybody got out by one o'clock, but you. I told her I have to walk my buddy home, and he's never had this much to drink, and she said stay, stay, sit down, watch tv and let him sleep it off a little…. Jesus! Who are you Theresa?"

Joe sat up, still next to her, and looked blankly into her bright brown eyes. He did not know what to say, but fully understood what Charles had just said. Maybe she had taken responsibility for her parents' house and did not drink or smoke at all, or what? "You don't have to say a word, Mister Joe Robinson. You know, I come to all your games at school. Know we are undefeated. Know you are our star. So, I want you in good shape for our first game of the new year next week. Go home with your friend who never showed how much beer he drank and get a good rest of the night's sleep."

Somehow Joe managed to return her smile, and as he slowly raised himself from the couch, all he could say was "thank you... thank you... thank you." During the walk home, Charles kept muttering something about unsophisticated kids while Joe could not stop thinking about Theresa. There was a hot spark there somewhere, but he could not place it, not understand it. It was a feeling. Could this be something sister Etta or Mom or better yet that Mama Sarah can explain? Before climbing into bed, Joe stared into the bathroom mirror, and for the first time, thought to himself: *You know, I'm not a bad looking guy, maybe even handsome.* And that he was.

**15**

"I just don't know. I just don't know. Hey, for the first time, I have to admit to you I'm very confused." Mama Sarah and Joe were sitting together on her living room couch in her house after dinner together. It was the evening before his start back to school ending the Christmas holiday. Joe had something he really wanted to tell her, but he deferred after her surprise opening statement.

"Ha, ha, that's really funny Mama, you confused. So okay, I'm your listening board now. Tell me, what's up, ma'am?"

"Well, you know I watch all this TV, flipping channels, some considered left wing, liberal, progressive, and a couple considered right wing, you know, conservative. So you and I have been talking about education a lot. Now that seems a subject both sides seem to agree on, kids need to grow up getting a good education. Good for our people, good for our economy, good for our country. Some say religious schools, charter schools, private schools… all do a better job at it. The side on the right, like the states with a majority Republican Party are passing the right for parents to chose schooling for their kids. The other side has public schools with very powerful unions behind the teachers that are resisting this.

So now what? Two different systems? Fighting, resentment? The move to school choice costs more money. It means more difficult physical transportation. It means some teachers resenting others. It means the big schoolteachers' unions standing up loud and clear against. It means that maybe a majority of kids, certainly in the Democratic Party areas, are left with weaker than ever public schools. My head is spinning young man. This certainly is not leading to national unity. Yes, yes, this is conflict. Conflict....

Her tone of voice now turned more positive. "I am so proud of you, young man. You are making a choice to stay in this so-called lousy public high school even though with your grades and your basketball talents you could get a scholarship out. I have to pray someone, somehow, will find an answer to this mess. They taught me long ago that every problem has a solution. I'm trying to teach you that conflict is an everyday situation.... You have your hands full, Joe, but you are going to do it."

"I hear you, Mama. I sure don't have an answer for you, but I promise you, I'm going to try...but can I try something else on you?" Joe was in a hurry to get this out to this wise old woman next to him. "We talk about problems, and we talk about conflict. Now I don't know what this is. That New Year's Eve party. Little wild but ended okay. Don't think anybody hurt. But me, yes, I learned. I drank too much beer and wine too fast. Know the legal age is 21 and here I'm 14, but the word around is everybody has to learn young, and at least we were in a house and not out on the streets. But, okay, I'm not going to do much of that if I think I'm going to get a basketball scholarship to college someday. But something else." Joe paused.

The serious faced Mama Sarah now softened her glance towards her great grandson, not quite believing this sudden burst into maturity.

"I think I'm with you Joe, Go on."

"Okay, okay, so a girl in my class, Theresa her name. Hardly ever noticed her at school. Well, the party was at her house, of course the parents away. Her older brother in charge. Well, she looked at me, and I looked at her. We danced a lot. We laughed a lot. She let me sleep it off a while after everybody else except Charles had gone. She looked at me again, told me she comes to all my home games. She talked to me, Mama, real nice, but all I could say was 'thank you'. Mama, I don't know how to handle this. What is this? I think I really like her."

"Spectacular, young man, spectacular. You sure are aggressive on the court and with your studies, but now you are in the new world of male/female, boy/girl. God has given us feelings, attractions to the opposite sex. After all, that's how we have been around and growing the last many thousands of years. Like anything else, exactly how we individually react to this because, as we talked before, we are all different, each and every one of us a unique individual. Obviously, she likes you, has difficult to describe feelings for you. You suddenly like her, have feelings for her you can't quite describe, put your finger on. The music, the dancing, that situation makes these attractions happen easier, faster.... Maybe Theresa is your first love, young man."

"Okay, I get it, but, but, Mama what do I do?"

"As they say, follow your heart. Maybe at school you look to pass her by and politely say 'hey, how you doing today'? And the next game, find her in the crowd with your eyes and give her a little smile. You know there will be more parties coming up. But be wise Joe. Yes, you will watch your drinking and you will stay away from the drugs, and you will continue your exercises. You are an athlete, Joe, the best." Joe felt relieved listening to mama's wisdom.

16

January and early February seemed to fly by while Joe's routine was the same. No matter how cold, unless it was raining or snowing, the playground ball on Saturdays and Sundays went full blast. If the weather was real bad, Joe would try to find good basketball or football games on the big William-bought TV in Mama Sarah's and MomMom Beatrices' living room. Charles was always invited and always came over. In school, hard practices run by Coach Smith were also welcomed by Joe. He continued to get stronger, bigger muscled and slightly taller, now reaching six feet. Joe's basketball team continued to excel with Joe leading the way. The team remained undefeated, and around school Coach Smith was talked about as a phenom. Joe was delighted to learn that Mr. Washington also taught African History, European History, and American History. He would sign up for each his next three years. He was learning so much taking World History this freshman year.

The only addition to Joe's routine was a delight. He and Theresa exchanged greetings every time they came close, at the end of a mutual class or in the hallways. Joe was sure to look for her at his home games, and she was there every time.

As February 14 approached, Joe heard about the controversy. It was rumored that what used to be an annual Valentine's Day dance in the school's gym, canceled several years ago because of too much surrounding violence and the detection of knives and guns, would be restored this year because the date fell on a Friday, and school security and even the school policemen would be backed up with additional personnel and security measures. Finally clarified on February 12, it was announced on the hallway bulletin boards the dance would be renewed and held in the gymnasium 8 pm to midnight with increased security measures, including searches and detectors at the main entrance to the school and again at just one entrance into the gym.

The day before the big event, Joe managed to stop Theresa in a hallway passing and utter something other than his typical greeting: "Hey, any chance you going to the dance Friday night?"

"You? If you go, I'll go. Be a lot of older kids there, but …." She smiled slightly, eyes wide open anxiously looking for Joe's response.

"For sure. Even if you go with your friends, I'll come by your house 8 o'clock and walk with you. Too much going on in our streets at night." She nodded in the affirmative as her smile grew even wider. "Okay, see ya," as they hustled on. Joe took a deep breath and felt really good about himself in that moment.

On Friday afternoon, the varsity team had a game away so the freshman team could stay on the floor until almost 5:30 and enjoy a little more shooting practice. Joe showered and quickly dressed in the locker room as he wanted to get home for dinner and then figure out what he would wear to the dance, and he did not want to be late to get over to Theresa's house by 8 pm. Both the jeans and the flannel shirt he wore to school that day surely would not do as both too small, and he had to consider that Mom had recently bought him some good fitting khaki pants and nice pullover sweater.

On his way home, he called Charles as the two had not confirmed any details about getting to the dance that night. "Charles, Charles, can you hear me? I'm walking home after practice. Can you come by my house by quarter to eight. We're going to meet Theresa at eight and walk her to the dance."

"Listen, bro, I told ya. I'm in this up to my eyeballs. Can't go. Look, I followed your wisdom, and I told my brother no drugs for me. And I told ya, cars, cars. I want you to come in with me and you keep resistin'. Tonight, I gotta make a delivery. I gotta get paid. No damn dance. Have fun with that new chick of yours."

"Charles, listen to me. It's supposed to rain tomorrow. No ball. You come over to my house, man, noon. You do it." Joe hung up and jammed his phone forcefully into his tight jean's pocket. His teeth tightened and he walked faster. To an outsider, this scene is what one would call stress, anxiety. His best friend: still looking for shortcuts in making money, and only 14 years old.

—m—

For Joe and Theresa, the night went just super great. Theresa had two girlfriends with her when Joe came by. They actually seemed grateful that Joe Robinson escorted them to the dance that evening. By now, he surely was well known by all in the freshman class for his outstanding basketball play and the undefeated freshman team. The two said few words at the dance but obviously enjoyed each other, especially when it came to the slow dances giving the two the chance for the first time to embrace. All went well fairly well inside, some pushing and shoving and loud cursing at times, but no major disorder. Security was tight and everyone of all high school ages plus the half dozen teacher chaperones kept things lively but fairly peaceful.

Not so outside. Despite the bright outside lights, it was not easy to miss the brawls, the marijuana smoke, the drug needles on the ground, some broken car windows. Security presence was limited outside as most attention was centered on inside the building. On Monday, the school principal in addressing his administrative staff and teacher staff remarked that the reinstatement of the Valentine's Day Dance was a fair success even though there had been quite a bit of disorder outside the gymnasium. It's a tough neighborhood he noted, which everyone he was addressing was obviously aware, and the situation would have to be reviewed again next year.

For Joe, the best part was the end of the evening. He accompanied Theresa's friends back to each one of their homes without an incident and then to her house. The porch light was on, but she unlocked the front door and turned it off. And then, their first kiss. Joe thought he was in heaven as he strolled home after their long embrace and probably a half dozen smiles and kisses. This is real life he thought to himself, the good part.

—⚏—

The next day was a real turnaround from the day before. It was a heavy cold rain that came in at daybreak, so no playground ball. Joe did an extra two sets of his strength building routine that morning before breakfast with Mom and Etta, and before he knew it Charles showed up around 11.

"Up to my room Charles, we gotta talk bro." But there, William was still in bed, although not unusual as he stays up so late most nights. "Let's go down to Etta's room, she's still downstairs with my mom.…. Look Charles, we talked before 'bout this," as the two sat down on the edge of Etta's bed. Charles tightened his face looking down as he well guessed what his friend wanted to talk about. Joe stared right at him. "Your father you tell me is a bastard. Your brother is in trouble half the time. My brother too. You tell me your brother can't get out of his drug gang probably without getting put down. Same thing with my brother. You know, bro, this illegal shit. Now you tell me your brother is also stealing cars. Ain't that illegal too, bro? So you wanna be a criminal? Yeah, I know all this Black Lives Matter shit. You're a juvenile. You ain't going to jail, and no bail anymore. The police are fallin' apart. So, you gonna get away with this shit, but not forever. It's gonna catch up with you someday, and you wanted me part of it?" Charles continued to look down, just waiting for his chance. "Well, you know that I decided not. I love basketball and I ain't doin' bad in school. For me, I'm choosing to get a college scholarship and not because I'm a poor black who needs a gift. I'm gonna earn it bro." Joe continued to look sternly at his buddy Charles but thought to himself: *Is this the same guy, my best friend? Am I getting through to him?*

Charles knew it was finally his turn. "Look man, you know I love you. We're tighter than brothers. I hear what ya sayin'. I don't have that basketball talent you have. Bro, you know that song 'I'm goin' nowhere, somebody help me.' Well I'm goin' nowhere and I ain't got nobody to help me. I got no wise old lady like you got to push me, to teach me. My family is a mess. Yeah, maybe I'll get plucked out as one of those underprivileged black kids, but I can't count on that Joe. So,

I stay in school in all the chaos and even graduate, then what? No good jobs here. Become a janitor making' minimum wage? Shit, man, I may as well just go for it. Take my chances." A pause, an opening for Joe.

"Charles, Charles, look at me. We're brothers, man. I love you too. We've hung out together since we were five years old. That so called kindergarten, what a joke. But look bro, play it straight, and I promise you, we'll develop your skills, your talents. I'll be with you. There are so many good trade schools, not round here but not far. You don't have to go to college, bro, but you can make a lot of money, carpenter, electrician, whatever. You can get smart and start your own company, Charles Plumbing Company. Sounds good. Get a nice house away from here. Build a family. Bring them all to my big house for Thanksgiving!" With that, the two began to laugh, relaxing, hugging each other…. True friendship.

—ɯ—

As the following days moved on, life was quite full for Joe. Basketball season was ending the last week in March. It was quite the buzz that this freshman basketball team was finishing its season undefeated. The last game coming up was one of the easiest, but Joe and Coach Smith were determined not to let up. No complacency was the word. Every weekend, Joe and Theresa continued their porch embracing, even moving to her living room couch when her parents were out, but Joe learned well. Mama Sarah's words, his sister's and his own mother's deeds. No time for 14-year-olds to get careless with sex. Respect for the girl's decency came before his new impulses.

The toughest part for Joe was his occasional exchange with brother William. Life certainly was not getting simpler or easier for him. He seemed upset and nervous at times while other times he was full of bravado, sounding tough, a real street fighter. He had hopes for friend Charles, but for William change seemed impossible. Joe hoped he could someday find a way to help him. For now, his big brother was not going to listen to his younger brother, someone who has never been out on the tough streets other than with all that simple playground ball.

—◦◦◦—

On April third, the miracle arrived. Etta had successfully fended off all the advice from her mother and grandmother and the so-called counselors they had her repeatedly visit. She prevailed, and within just three hours after heading to the hospital after her water broke, baby Arlene was born. Six pounds, ten ounces, and perfectly healthy. Joe now had a baby niece. Etta had diligently prepared a nursery area in her little bedroom. The two were going to be quite happy together.

Joe felt a sense of joy, but also felt that he wanted to engage with Mama Sarah now that 17-year-old Etta, with a child to raise, still had to find a productive path forward in life and not be completely dependent on other family members and on government welfare.

And reflecting on births and birthdays with Etta and Arlene, it was Joe's turn next. Two weeks after Arlene's debut, on April 17th, Joe celebrated his 15th birthday. Not only his whole female family but even William, sang Happy Birthday to him around a cake with fifteen candles. Both Charles and Theresa showed up for the grand occasion. Amidst the guns, the drugs, the violence, there were still times of joy in these poor, underprivileged, underserved communities.

# 17

It was Sunday evening in early May with the whole family enjoying their typical delicious Sunday dinner when MomMom Beatrice announced "No one leave the table. I have something important to say." The apple pie dessert was finished, and this was the usual time Beatrice and Ella started clearing the table and William would disappear. On this evening, Etta, who had been holding baby Arlene with one hand and eating with the other, gave a look of surprise and proceeded to place a pacifier in her young child's mouth and sat still. William looked disturbed but after pushing his chair back remained seated. "Okay, now want I want to tell you is that my good friend Nell down the street has talked to me about joining her organization. I have to make up my mind this week, but I want you all to know first before neighbors here start buzzin' all kinds of stuff about us. It's called BLM Philly, Black Lives Matter." Mama Sarah and Mom Ella sat up erect, a look of astonishment on their faces.

"Now, now, nobody get excited. Let me tell you, these people want to create a loving society, get rid of police brutality, get our schools teaching Black history, get more Black teachers into our schools. They been doin' a lot of good even though they call themselves 'radical'. I think I can help them. Blacks are now 50% of the population here, and they tellin' me Philadelphia has the highest poverty in the whole country of any big city, 12% of white are poor but 25% of black poor. Politicians ain't fixin' it, so we gotta do it."

"Now wait, mother," interrupted Ella. "I've been approached too, but what you say is only half true. They got big attention a few years ago with the shootin' of several black folks. No doubt police forces have some bad apples and not enough done to weed out the bad ones. But these folks want to not just cut back spending on police forces, but like you say they are admittedly radical, want to disrupt society with something completely different. They want to get rid of police altogether, and even jails. They believe everybody can be good and love and that we don't need families anymore, just loving communities, but look at what's going on, a few white cops shooting a Black kid but so many, many, many more young Blacks shooting other Blacks, and now even shooting innocent cops. It's crazy!"

William leaned back on his chair and smiled. "Hey MomMom, good news. Get rid of all the cops."

"Now let me jump in here," Mama Sarah interrupted. You know I watch TV all day and look at my laptop computer that William kindly bought me. I know all about this BLM, daughter dear. I have studied their website carefully. I see the conflict that's going on. They have what they call a Vision.

It's very incoherent and confusing. They want a Black utopia. Then they have a Mission, again very incoherent. They feel so many Blacks feel marginalized, and Black Power will fix it. Then they have about a dozen Guiding Principles which becomes Heaven on Earth.... Now I agree dear daughter that if you simplify all this and start with the basics of ways to eliminate instances of police brutality, getting more Black history taught, more good Black teachers, get better mental health approaches, less discrimination, better counselors, but very importantly we need an economy for all, jobs for our young Blacks. BLM never mentions that word 'economy'. You can't have society success without economic success.

"So, I say improve don't destroy. What these folks are missing is that we are not all born saints, and they think we have been mistreated. They do not understand human nature. We have many who are going to be disorderly and need discipline and yes punishment of some form when the rules are broken." She glanced at William, who was no longer smiling. "I see the debate. I understand their pain. Yes, be forceful, unrelenting in your efforts to make change, to fix the past with a brighter future. But understand the other side. There is a young Black, Attorney General of the state of Kentucky, running for governor. He stands for law and order. He believes in advancement on merit not this DEI stuff. There is another Black, already the Governor of Maryland. He was raised in tough Baltimore, but his mom was resourceful, unrelenting, and got him into the Valley Forge Military Academy. He tried to escape back to the Baltimore streets but was restrained. He was very bright, like our Joe here. He advanced into the military and colleges. He learned the value of discipline. He excelled. He met the right people and now look at him and yes, he is on the side of the progressive liberal left, but he is on the side of helping, of solving the problem, not creating chaos. And chaos, look at what happened with all the looting here, all over Philadelphia by young people, and some against Black store owners. Law and order yes, with police and law enforcement yes, but at the same time someone has to fix the problem why these young people act as they do. Look, we have tons of individuals, organizations, schools, universities, hospitals each helping out, trying to correct the problems of discrimination and inequities. God bless them. Each does a good job for those they picked out, but it's the few not the many who are being helped."

"You got that mother? Ya gotta look at both sides and come up with somethin' better," interjected Ella. "Look, when I walk home at night, I want to feel safe. I keep lookin' over my shoulder. William here knows all bout that. We need an honest police force. We don't need all these guns goin' off and all this lootin'."

William now raised himself from his chair and slowly walked out of the room. Etta looked a bit confused and turned her attention to baby Arlene. Joe sat still mesmerized, wanting to hear more, wondering in his mind how all of this was going to turn out someday. MomMom Beatrice, the 60-year -old grandmother, and now great grandmother to the newest member of the family, sat still, befuddled, not clear in her mind about all of this 'both sides' stuff. She started thinking to herself. She remembered her mother, Sarah, talking to the three kids, about a balance of love and discipline, that her two brothers listened well and are off somewhere West doing very well, and here she is just biding her time, never paid any attention, living off the government's generous benefits and William's illicit dollars, and now completely confused about what she does next, and what to tell friend Nell. She thought about watching television and seeing all the good- looking Black newscasters, weather people, and all the ads featuring a Black husband, a Black wife, a Black kid in a nice suburban home. Lordy, you would think the Blacks are 60% of the population not our 13%. Guess they all went to college and being shown to be successful and be just like the whites. So, are we all are supposed to feel better? But there are plenty of poor whites, and lordy there are so many more of us Blacks not living like those TV Blacks. *I am really confused,* she thought to herself.

*More conflict,* thought Joe.

Spring moved on. Even those who pushed for Etta to have an abortion were delighted to have little baby Arlene in their lives now. Etta took full charge of her baby's daily affairs. The only favor she asked was for her mom or grandmom to pick up some diapers and baby food when they were out shopping. William continued his late nights out and was extremely quiet whenever he was home for dinner. When he did bump into Joe in their bedroom morning or night, he simply grumped, complained, and cursed out loud about his gang matters. Joe could offer no advice.

Joe was doing fine for the most part. He did his schoolwork, continuing to earn great grades. He continued with his daily strength building routines, his joining up with Theresa on Friday and Saturday evenings despite his buddy Charles telling him he was spending too much time with her and therefore missing some great parties. He was back to playground basketball after school and on weekends during the day. He enjoyed his brief encounters with the one teacher so inspiring to him, Mr. Washington. His "chats" with Mama Sarah were occurring less often and were fairly quiet. He was getting the hint that she was now looking to him for finding some answers to life's complexities.

Where he was suffering was, as usual, in the area of trying to make sense of all the conflicts around him. Bullying, fighting, and even occasional gunshots at the playground continued. Joe was so strong and good on the court that he had earned and deserved respect from the older tough guys. Nobody got too rough with him as he dribbled up and down the court deftly passing and scoring many baskets. Same in the school lunchroom as he now was known as the basketball star who had led the freshman basketball team to an astonishing undefeated record. But the chaos there and in the classrooms continued. Yelling out loud, interrupting teachers, selling drugs, disrespecting girls, some pushing and shoving, all were common occurrences. If something really got way out of hand, a student was expelled from school, but that form of punishment seemed to mean nothing as that student was not serious about learning anyway.

—ɷ—

So, conflict, conflict, conflict, conflict. And two black worlds. The one - the small minority in good homes with young kids starting school off with love and discipline. Older kids getting into good charter schools and private schools and some getting college scholarships, some based on merit, and some based on "diversity, equity and inclusion". Then there was the wide array of spirited institutions, organizations, and generous individuals helping so many black kids. The public school district offering so many extra services to the school kids. Many kids completing college and moving into good jobs.

And then to number two in the black world - the larger group, the so called "poor, underserved, underprivileged" black kids in these deteriorating neighborhoods that were full of guns, drugs, and crime. No politician or black leader had solved this bad situation in the last 50 years, said Mama Sarah. And she had told Joe that government handouts and criminal leniency had not helped either, probably made it worse.

Our Joe Robinson had to do some deep thinking, and he did.

# PART TWO

PART TWO

# 1

Joe Robinson graduated from high school with high honors, a first team award on the city's Public All-League Basketball selection, a steady, beautiful girlfriend named Theresa, a best friend named Charles who had not yet been arrested for selling all his stolen goods to the Mexican cartels or getting apprehended for his car stealing, an older brother not yet shot in his gang travails, an aging great grandmother who could not hide her pride in this young man, a struggling part time working grandmother and a hardworking, socially active mother ever arguing, a lovely sister with an energetic, joyful, young child, a surrogate father in history teacher Ron Washington, and most exciting for Joe a full four-year athletic scholarship to a basketball powerhouse college, Villanova University.

But just prior to entrance, Joe had a new troubling thought, one he was losing a lot of sleep over. Playing basketball was terrific for him personally, but to do so would not be helping the cause he had sworn to Mama Sarah he would devote his life to: the mission of trying to find a way to help those left behind in his Black community. So, at the last-minute Joe decided to accept the academic scholarship offered to him by the University of Pennsylvania, a city school founded by the great Benjamin Franklin, a top Ivy League college with the multiple resources which might just help him find the answers.

Joe was moving on. He continued with his strength building and basketball skills but now also with his intellect. Not only had Joe done a lot of thinking about conflict over the last three years of high school but had also learned a lot of action steps towards solving difficulties. Joe learned the Problem/Solution approach. P/S. He took the optimistic approach that every problem has a solution. He learned that while every person has a different brain further differentiated by situations starting in the mother's womb like smoking and diet, differences in individual biology, early childhood environment, a multitude of growing up influences; that still, it seemed to Joe that every child thrives on a proper balance of love and discipline. That there is a logical explanation for the myriad differences in people's behaviors, but that there are some basics. That historically there is good behavior and bad behavior, defined by a person's legal and cultural norms, and that good behavior is normally rewarded, and bad behavior is punished, the extent again varying to the times and to a person's legal and cultural system. But no matter the society, if there was a Problem with behavior, the Solution was rewarding the good behavior and punishing the bad behavior.

And again, that a proper balance of love and discipline was a rock-solid foundation for good human behavior.

He went on to study the problems. The history of slavery was worldwide but to some in the United States, the sorrowful legacy continued on. Legally abolished in 1865, but followed by massive discrimination practices in schools, housing, restaurants, transportation, jobs etc., then followed by legal rights in voting in 1965, along with better job hiring, Southern college admittance, and in many other areas. Some still believed that Blacks are 'victims', that 'white supremacy' still rules while others believe that Black culture, that is Black norms, values and beliefs, is the problem not white supremacy, that such a culture is the way of Black living norms in many areas, while others see the lack of job opportunities and missing fathers in many black neighborhoods the major cause of crime and drugs. Joe realized this was not such a simple problem to define let alone resolve. Not a simple P/S scenario. To Joe, a CONFLICT in capital letters.

Drugs, guns, crime, police brutality, lack of home and school discipline, male testosterone in young Black men, missing fathers at home, ongoing white supremacy, insufficient teaching of Black history, poorly maintained neighborhoods, lack of kindergarten and first grade orderliness in Black schools, poor results of city high schools, discrimination in jobs, insufficient job opportunities, division among even Blacks in defining the problems and solutions, self-promoting politicians, too many government handouts, growing disparities between "successful" Blacks and "poor" Blacks, too many Blacks in jails compared to whites, too many abortions of Black babies compared to white – Joe's list of the Problems had grown quite long. How in the world could he come up with an S to each of these P's?

One of Joe's top priorities was addressing the problem of a lack of rewarding jobs available to Black high school graduates in the Philadelphia region. With his love of history, his college major of course was History, Penn's program ranking #3 in the whole country. He had learned that through most of the 19$^{th}$ century, North Philadelphia had been the nation's industrial and commercial powerhouse. Lots of output, locomotives, subway cars, textiles; lots of skilled jobs. And then decline after the World Wars. The unionized textile industry moving South, new methods of transportation like automobiles to Detroit, and so on. Outside of the growing health care industry and center city historical sites, Philadelphia declined in fame and population while growing in unkept "poor" neighborhoods.

Through Joe's initiative in taking some elective courses in Penn's #1 in the nation Wharton Business School, he found a way to meet up with a young billionaire Wharton grad. Joe presented the Problem and offered the grad a Solution to the Jobs issue. SHOES! Everybody wears them, have a number of them, and need to continually replace them. A perfect market, a growing market in a nation with population growth in all categories and a nation of wealth offering a great variety of footwear. Joe picked Athletic and Casual – two with the fastest growth and most variety. He studied the market. It was there. It was open to something new, or revised versions of old favorites. He studied the production. It was now varied and changing after many years of similar production methods. He studied the players. Since labor costs were so low in Asia [China at $6/hr., Vietnam $3/hr.] the largest company in this niche NIKE made all their shoes over there, 96 of its 100 suppliers located in Vietnam. Low duties and low transportation costs for large volumes were also favorable.

Joe studied them all. In the United States, a number of small companies produced various kinds of shoes in low volumes. Some made in Los Angeles, some in Oregon and Seattle. A well-known American company New Balance, a private company with a headquarters in Boston and one fifth the volume of NIKE, made most of its athletic shoes in China, a few in the U.K., and produced some sneakers made in five facilities in Maine and Massachusetts. Another U.S. company, publicly owned Skechers headquartered in Manhattan Beach, California, showed remarkable growth and marketing strategies boasting from zero sales in 1993 to over $7 billion in 2022 with a robust 48% gross margin and 8% operating margin. But as Joe duly noted, all of its shoes were manufactured in China and Vietnam. And so on, like the big name North Face athletic shoes, mostly made overseas.

Another big name Joe found was the European company Adidas and learned of their innovations. Since most producers had to buy some 30 different components to put together their finished product at an assembly factory, it was stated it took an average of 60 days to accumulate everything and then an average of 50 hours to produce one shoe. Adidas found ways to shorten this process by creating their 'Adidas Speedfactory' by attempting to make all the components in one place and by introducing labor saving devices using robots.

So Joe thought: a huge growing market fulfilling everyone's needs forever with great variety, a labor intensive industry, and one open to technological innovation. He also could show in his planned presentation to the Wharton billionaire that the industry can be profitable: NIKE with its multitude of competitors showing almost $30 billion in sales with a 45% gross margin after production costs and a 10% net profit margin.

Joe then analyzed the economics of an athletic shoe, a lower cost one like at $70 retail. The cost of the 23 major components, the upper combined at 34% of the total, the labor and overhead at 27%, the outsole bottom at 14%, the packing, and the minor rest – all combined to only $15. Add $2 for shipping, customs and insurance to $17. The producer then sells to the retailer at $35, double the cost to earn a 50 percent gross profit. The retailer doubles the cost to $70 hoping to make over 45% gross after promotions and discounts and unsold inventory. In his example Joe figured the labor at only $4 per shoe so no wonder the big shoe companies are not producing expensive shoes in the United States where minimum wages are being demanded at $15 to $25 an hour compared to Vietnam at $3 hr. and shipping in volume at only $.50 per pair of shoes. A Philadelphia producer would have to be innovative enough to create a lot of jobs but keep total labor costs in line in order to be competitive.

Joe thought long and hard as to how and when to make his presentation. He read every printed piece coming out of the Wharton School during his senior year. He learned when the billionaire's class was coming back to Penn for a reunion. He learned who had responded affirmative to the invitations and where and when they would be meeting. He thought of various ways he could pull an introduction and how he would introduce himself. He knew in advance he would be graduating with high honor awards and first team All-IVY in basketball, and he made it a point to get friendly with his Wharton Finance course professor who might very well introduce this honor student and basketball star. But most of all it was about how to prepare his Pitch and then leave with the billionaire a very concise, easy to read Business Plan spelling out the current duress of the black Philadelphia neighborhoods with its potential to hire thousands of just out of high school and college, the so called 'underprivileged' who would have a positive attitude towards hard work, trade school training provided by the new enterprise, start at minimum wages, eager for pay raise promotions based on time and merit, and for the spirit of making the Philadelphia Shoe the biggest and best in the United States. Joe's Business Plan would also incorporate knowledge about all the help that Penn and Wharton would give to these young adults along with the vast improvements in high school achievements lead by a reinvigorated Public School District and its leaders. All the billionaire had to do was believe it, to follow Joe's tips on where to find cost cutting tips on innovative ways to improve shoe making technology along with Joe's ideas about finding cost savings to be competitive with cheap overseas labor, to be pro-active, pro-American, and to open his wallet. Yes, The Philadelphia Shoe Company, Inc. producing "Philly's Best", a wide variety of athletic and casual wear shoes for the entire nation, a company producing job opportunities and advancements for young Philadelphians, a company with skilled counselors available to manage personal conflicts, a company with its own trade school, a company providing free family health care, a company offering stock grants for just a few years of satisfactory and good performance, a company attracting star Philadelphia pro athletes and celebrities for promotion, a company whose best performers would attract college scholarships in the evenings from the region's top universities. A real winner.

But there was one more thing. The kids in school had to be convinced that graduating and going to trade school, college, or taking a job like at the new shoe company was going to be personally rewarding, to their personal advantage. Joe remembered clearly what Mama Sarah had taught him. We tend to behave in a way that is to our advantage, each individual unique, each interpretating that personal advantage in different ways. But of course, there are some commonalities.

So, one evening after his evening 'workout", Joe retreated to his Mom's dining room table with two large books – a Webster's dictionary and a Webster's thesaurus that Mama had gifted him as his high school graduation present. He remembered Mama's words about children needing a balance of love and discipline, that society needs to be orderly in order to thrive, and that tight families are the best means in achieving this outcome. But Joe knew clearly that these ideal conditions are rare in his part of town. What was needed to succeed? So, he looked up the word "motivation". His mind raced. *That's what we need!* Why did I spend summers spending so much time and effort on the playground basketball court? Why did I pay attention to my schoolwork and get all A's. Why did William quit school and turn to drugs? Why did my buddy Charles turn to stealing? Why was Theresa so nice to everyone?

The words of definition were many. Motivation – the act or process to impel, excite, force, influence, drive; an impulse, incentive, spur; a stimulus to action, an emotion or desire operating on the will to act; a driving power, a stimulus that increases energy, to move into action; a catalyst, impetus, impulse, stimulant, incentive.

Okay, he thought, I've got it. Let's just say it's an internal force causing me to act in a certain way. The way we were raised, our environment, our unique brain chemistries are all going to cause us to behave in a different way. Mama Sarah's stern moral teachings were a great influence on me. We didn't go anywhere in the summer so all the playground time was obvious. My reading of the football star Hershel Walker's exercises played a big impact on my physical development. Mr. Washington's approach to learning caught my immediate attention. William, Charles - I could just feel inside the difference between right and wrong. Theresa – I just could feel that I must have luckily met the right girl. These were "incentives', "inducements", but there must be something else. Yes, it's that these influences must be different in their power. In each individual, some must be weak, or moderate, or strong.

Joe looked up, puzzled. So then, to make this idea of a new industry creating jobs a success, there must be a strong motivation for kids in high school to graduate, to achieve something good for themselves, to want to become part of a good society. How in the world do we accomplish this amidst the crime, drugs, and guns? How could we accomplish this if there is not a Mama Sarah or a strong father around?

# PART THREE

PART THREE

1

"Com'on Mama, tell us again how Uncle Joe did it. Please...."

"Oh, lordy me, Arlene. I've told you so many times, but okay, your Mommy is here too, so let's do it again."

Mama Sarah had just turned a remarkable 96 years of age. Her diet was good and she made sure she walked every single day for exercise, changing a several trips a day up and down stairs to a walk around the block now that the street outside was safer and cleaner. She also thought to herself that she must have inherited good genes. Lately however, she noticed a steep decline in her stamina yet did not want to see a doctor, check her pulse or her blood pressure. Nevertheless, she was still a happy person knowing she had been a good influence on young Joe's life, and now she could enjoy her "chats" with this darling young ten year old great great granddaughter, even a more special delight now that Arlene's mother, twenty seven year old Etta, had been convinced by Joe to go back to high school, earn a diploma and then land a nice job at the Philadelphia Shoe Company where brother Joe was quite a large shareholder, the youngest officer and director anyone could ever imagine. Joe Robinson was only 25 years old.

Lately however, Mama noticed her stamina had declined but still strong enough to carry on these conversations.

"Well, I'll tell you, young Miss Arlene. Your Uncle Joe and his billionaire friend, oh I cannot for the life of me ever remember how to pronounce his name right. That little company they started, well, it's growing leaps and bounds, and already it's the talk of the business folks all around the whole country. A real success story. But you know that from your mommy.

"Yea, yea, I know, Mama. Go on, all the other stuff."

"Yes, yes, young lady. Let's get this right."

"Sorry, I know, good English. Yes, yes."

"Okay, my dear, it's Saturday. You have no school today, and your mom not working, and it's raining out, so I guess we have all afternoon."

Arlene sat up in the comfortable couch in Mama Sarah's living room with some soft lights on amidst some real nice furniture she learned had been bought by Uncle William some years ago. She was all ears as she leaned against this wise old woman with the aged skin but still bright eyes.

"So your Uncle Joe and I used to talk a lot about the natural human condition of conflict. It's part of our human nature dear, the situation where two people, two groups, two nations just cannot see eye to eye. They simply disagree, and the result may be war, shooting, physical fighting, verbal or written arguing, compromising where no one gets all they want but they resolve things peacefully, amicably. Win/lose or win/win or lose/lose, all combinations. Have any of that at school, dear, or on your cell phone, or the movies you watch?"

"Yes, Mama, I do. Why is that? Why can't we all just get along?"

"Ha, young lady. Many years ago, a person accused of being a criminal but who didn't really want to be a criminal asked that same simple question. But the answer is also simple. Oh my, this is all stuff I talked about with your Uncle Joe long ago, but okay, let me do it again. Your mommy here might like to hear it too.

"We humans of the big brain have been around a long time, maybe 300,000 years? But each of our big brains is incredibly complex and don't all work the same. We are each an individual creation and each influenced by tons of different biology and events.... Now it's a blessing dear to be so unique, but yes that uniqueness does create differences of thoughts and actions. And we can be born to be quite disorderly. That complexity is what creates conflict. You see dear, you will learn in school that we humans with the bigger brains than other mammals have been around for hundreds of thousands of years, but we became what we call civilized only ten thousand years ago. That's when we cultivated foods, developed languages, domesticated animals like sheep, goats, and cows. Before that, all that time, our brains had worked in a way to force us to respond to threatening events, like someone trying to steal our food, by being violent. It was necessary to survive. Other times, our brains forced us to be cooperative with others in order to better the common good. We tended to behave which either way based upon what we thought to be to our own advantage. And what's so amazing is that it is easy and natural for the **same** person at times to be quite calm and cooperative with others but at other times to become quite violent – all depending upon their upbringing, their mental health, and combined with the current circumstances right in front of them. You will learn in school about the 'fight or flight' response. And you will see in everyday life, in the violent movies conflict is resolved by physical fighting and by guns and knives or by running away. In the romantic movies the mounting conflict is resolved at the end by true love. In our democratic governments like America, conflict is resolved by compromises and by majority voting. On our streets, conflict is resolved by those breaking a law by going to jail. And in our homes and in our schools, conflict occurs everyday and often does not get resolved and goes on with yelling, arguing, threatening, or bullying.... So, that is the simple answer to your question dear, 'why can't we all just get along'?" Arlene's mouth dropped.

"Golly, is this stuff too deep, dear? Oh well. Anyway, let's go on. Your Uncle Joe. He has devoted his young life to resolving all those some twenty problems in our poor Black communities, resolving those natural and neighborhood conflicts but in a way without resorting to violence. Are you with me so far?"

"Think I understand, Mama. Don't stop," answered Arlene. Etta smiled and nodded her head affirmative.

—∿∿—

The ensuing conversation soon became a long monologue. Three hours in duration, with young Arlene occasionally falling off to sleep a few moments, but never letting go of snuggling up to her great great grandmother and holding her arm. Trying to fully understand what this wise old woman was saying. Her mother, Etta, sat still entranced.

"Okay, so you understand the importance of working, like your Mommy here, so we can go to the store and buy our foods to eat and pay our bills, like for our TV. I wonder if I told you how your Uncle Joe did that. Now from there, Uncle Joe had to deal with all this conflict stuff I have been telling you about. We are not going to settle the big conflicts like the disputes among countries that go to war against each other, or the violent conflicts shown in the movies and on TV to attract so many viewers, but Joe set out to deal with the many conflicts right here on our home front. Before he graduated from college, he went to the Penn president and made a passionate plea to have the university do two things. First, to have Penn professors form a task force to develop a mandatory program for kindergarten teachers to learn methods for gaining the attention of their little students, with themes of balancing love and discipline, of learning that 'yes' means 'yes' and 'no means 'no', of ways to show the kids that their teachers care for them, that they are there to learn, of various ways to reward good behavior and various non-violent ways to punish bad behavior. Now we know professional counselors are trained to do something similar but there is no way there can be a trained counselor sitting in every classroom every day. Penn accepted the idea, and it's been working great the last three years since it began with the Philadelphia School District fully behind it. It was many years ago that Penn had declared a responsibility to its neighborhood, and the university did help several nearby schools, some problems but mostly successful. And its nearby neighbor, Children's Hospital did start a Behavior Center to help nearby neighborhood kids, but Joe's efforts were intended for the entire city, for all Philadelphia kids.

"Second, the Penn professors would form another task force and develop two more programs. Our American big companies and many of our universities have developed many programs targeting conflict management and conflict resolution, but most all for employees. These deal with the means of negotiation, the use of a mediator, a listener who hears all sides, steers a middle course of compromise so that all parties come up with something they can live with. Now here in our schools, such programs would have to be a little tighter, a little firmer because in our neighborhoods and in our schools often the conflicts lead to physical violence. So for 7th graders entering junior high school, Joe's ideas were a mandatory introductory course in Conflict Management, then entering high school in 9th grade the mandatory course would be Conflict Resolution, emphasizing ways to resolve conflict without resorting to violence. The School District was fully behind Penn's help and reinstructed its counselors to work with every 7th and 9th grade teacher in mastering this instruction. As far as Joe tells me, the program has gotten off to a great start and earning plaudits around the country."

Little Arlene could not understand every word Mama Sarah was saying, but she did grasp the meaning, as almost every day, just in her 4th grade at grammar school, she did witness all kinds of disputes, carrying-ons, like yelling, pushing, shoving, fights. And her Uncle Joe was helping with all this. Etta sat still, but she did listen and understand every word Mama Sarah was saying. She remained silent, feeling a sense of pride in her family, and she couldn't wait to hear more.

"Sit tight, you two. I need to get a glass of water. I'm talking so much."

"Stay, Mama, I'll get it," said Etta as Mama Sarah now seemed to look and act quite tired.

Moments later the monologue continued. "Okay, you two,

let's go over all the types of conflict our boy addressed while getting the great shoe company going and getting our great Ben Franklin's great University of Penn partnering with our now great Philadelphia School District." She nodded and smiled at that last comment.

"First, **drugs**. So Etta, your grandmother, my dear daughter Beatrice, you know she had gotten involved with Black Lives Matter Philly, sort of half-heartedly, but at least in tune with some of what they are trying to do for our Black society. Well, Joe had her introduce him to the higher ups there, and he used some of the words in their Mission statement like 'Youth Development' and their Guiding Principles statement like 'Collective Value' to point out that these strong drugs are ruining too many young Black lives and leading to much violence Black on Black. And he referred to their motto of being 'radical'. Well, he argued, for too many years the War on Drugs had failed. It's time to get radical. Push the City of Philly to get really tough with the dealers, get motivators in the schools to more aggressively teach kids the bad outcomes of taking drugs, train counselors how to better get the message across, actually come up with novel ways to punish the drug dealers. Well, you know, Joe's push really did a lot of good. No way to get rid of the increasingly legal marijuana, but immediately there was a vast improvement in getting rid of the really bad stuff off our streets. It was all a bottoms-up approach instead of a top down. The whole community got behind the movement."

Etta nodded her head in approving understanding. "Is that how my brother William ended up working for Philly Shoes and got off the street?"

"Right," replied Sarah. "And just in time before the law caught up with him as part of a dealer gang." Arlene looked puzzled by talk she didn't understand.

—⁕—

"Okay, **guns.** So Joe knew with three hundred million people in the country but four hundred million guns, most constitutionally protected, there was no way to get rid of them, but why not appeal to the joy of winning the lottery. He convinced his billionaire friend, who then convinced some of his rich friends along with several of the big Philly charities to put this program in place: for each gun turned in to the city, and no penalty for illegal guns, the giver would receive $1000, but then each 25th person would receive $25,000. Wow! Money talks! Thousands of guns have been turned in, and the program continues. Not a cure all, but its success continues, and kids, I can wander down our street now without fear of taking a random shot!

"So, **crime.** You do know about this, you two. Around the time you were born Arlene, your mother and I watched

TV every night and all we were seeing and hearing was the increasing crime rate. Stealing from stores, stealing cars. Police activity declining, police recruitment declining, prosecutions falling. And yes, even our BLM folks pushing hard to get rid of the police altogether seemed a little perplexed. So Joe's answer was, sure, reform the police and get the bad actors out but recognize the Black people living on these streets, working in, or owning, some of these stores and cars need and want protection from crime. Remember, I preached we can be very disorderly in our human nature, and we need some rules of behavior. So Joe went to City Hall with a bunch of Black store owners with him and laid out the case to our new, smart Mayor that the city needs a strong District Attorney's office to prosecute the breaking of any law, no more minor offenses going free. And if the jails serving as punishment for doing wrong are failing or overcrowded, Joe presented a whole book load of ideas, like improved work programs, rehab programs, and educational programs that he had gathered from the most successful around the country. Your punishment was loss of freedom from society, but you would be a much better person when you were released. Seems like Joe's efforts have really paid off. Our streets around here are so much more peaceful and cleaner. And our mayor, always outspoken against lawlessness, and our city officials are doing such a better job. Breaking the law in any respect is punishable while at the same time we have greatly improved our rehabilitation programs. And also at the same time, the police unions have been persuaded to take prompt action against their officers not living up to set standards – no more cries of police brutality."

"Could that be why there are now more Black fathers in the home, Mama?" said Etta. Arlene looked up startled. In the back of her mind she must have wondering all over again just who was her father.

"Yes dear. Most folks agree that the role of the **family** is one of the most important factors in the success of any society, and …."

"Mama Sarah, say no more. In my twenty-six years of life here, you have been the cement that holds our family together. Our Sunday dinners together, with even William enjoying them, have been our blessing. You have been so full of wisdom for us all. We would be lost without you. Joe is right, we have to get our fathers back." Tears came to Etta's eyes as she spoke her heart. Sarah looked down with a soft smile on her aging face. In her mind she must have been reflecting that now, thankfully, Joe is taking her place.

"Right dear, Joe has been instrumental in creating motivations for fathers to be home…. Okay, ladies, had enough?"

"No, no," retorted both Etta and Arlene together. "Tell us everything, Mama," said Etta.

"Hmmm, okay, we have talked about the importance of

home and family values. Two areas Joe has pushed hard on. So let's go back to conflict a little bit more, and how **school discipline** has been such a problem for so many years. I told you about programs that Joe pushed on dealing with conflict management and conflict resolution for students coming into junior high school and high school and for programs for kids coming into kindergarten and first grade to learn the difference between 'yes' and 'no', and how important our University of Pennsylvania and our Philadelphia School District leaders and our mayor have been in this effort. But what I didn't tell you was that every single week Joe takes an hour off work to visit a different school and speak about what we are and what we can become. He gives examples of how we are born quite disorderly by our very nature. Put ten boys or ten girls in a room for fifteen minutes with no adults around and no direction as to what the kids should be doing and take a motion picture with sound. Complete chaos! The students Joe is talking to all burst out in laughter as Joe acts this scene out. He then describes a group of Army recruits the first week they are in basic training. Standing at attention, getting yelled at, complete discipline. Why? Because the training of discipline leads one to learning the required sense of self-discipline when the going gets tough on the battlefield. Joe then leads into the need for early discipline, the enforcement of rules, of good behavior, all because life proceeds with the need to better oneself, to learn that orderliness makes life worthwhile. Why be a dumb kid yelling in the classroom? Where is that going to lead you? What's next? Hoping that the rich people or the government will take care of you? Turning to crime to make a living? Joe tells me he doesn't know the percentage, but he is sure a good number get the message.... And you know, ladies, sometimes he talks about the boy/girl situation. Couple more years Arlene and your mother will be talking to you about this. About boys have hormones, inside chemicals, that make them stronger in their teenage years and which can lead them to be aggressive physically and also to have stronger feelings towards girls, while the girls develop hormones that allow them to have babies. Without restraints, you know rules of behavior, right Etta, we have so many young pregnant girls."

Etta squinted her eyes hearing this and stared hard at her great grandmother, but she knew Mama was right. "But, Mama, things are getting so much better. I know the school counselors are so much better now talking to the kids about sex. We know that Blacks in America are 13% of the population but were 40% of the abortions, and that a big shot politician once argued for unlimited abortions because restrictions would mean too many poor kids being born. Ha! But Mama, in Philadelphia now with this better education, better politicians, better Black communities, better methods of pregnancy prevention, we have really cut down on what I went through.... And I know Joe has been part of all this too."

With a nod of approval, Sarah smiled warmly at Etta and then moved on. "Now you know, your brother, Etta, and your uncle, Arlene, he has become more than just a strong force in our neighborhoods around here. You know he always hated the terms 'poor, underprivileged, underserved, victims' all those names people were calling us. Some were saying it was our lousy 'culture' holding us back. Others were saying it was 'white supremacy' keeping us down. So, when the so called 'liberal, progressives' started their programs to help us, you know 'diversity, equity, inclusion' some of us moved quite easily into mainstream America, and a lot of people took pats on their backs for that, but the truth was the **majority of us** especially in the big cities still lived in rundown neighborhoods living on Medicaid health care and Food Stamps. Well, Joe has been writing magazine articles about that. Long before there was real white supremacy mainly due to the white Europeans a couple hundred years ago developing educational institutions, better weapons, and better ships, there was Persian supremacy, Egyptian supremacy, Mongolian supremacy, Aztec supremacy – many different people of different colored skins at their time of dominance. Yes, America settled by white Europeans subjected the red natives and the black slaves, but that dominance ended legally over 60 years ago. Joe says let's get on with it. Blacks are now in key political positions, advancing in top colleges and in business, so Joe says learn history you kids, keep your Black traditions at home but assimilate into this great American society. Sure, there are legal anti-discrimination rules galore, and lots of new opportunities, and be just as surely, there will be some who will always have a built-in animosity for anyone with a different colored skin or nationality. But Joe says to us: **Be Philadelphian, be American! Learn well, work hard, and advance on your merits....** You know ladies, I think his writings are making a big impact. I won't be around, but I just wonder where our Joe will be in this society ten years from now. He Is a miracle."

Little Arlene popped her head up. "I know what miracles are, Mama. That's Uncle Joe?"

"Think so little one. Can you get your Mama another glass of water. I'm talking so much."

—⁂—

"Well, little one, let's rehash and end up. Ten years ago before you were born, things were really a mess around here. Your mother had dropped out of high school, your Uncle William was involved in a drug gang, your grandmother Ella and great grandmother Beatrice worked hard to bring a little money into a home with no grown men around. We really didn't like the government handouts and William's drug money, but we had little choice. The politicians then were of no help. We had too many Blacks in our jails and too many divisions among our so-called Black leaders. Philadelphia with its 20% poverty rate was the worst big city in the entire United States. Only 9% of Black workers had a higher income than the 50% median income of white workers. Our public schools were so bad that taking out the private and charter schools, only a little over 60% of the kids graduated. We had high crime and poor policing and prosecution. We had few good job opportunities for Blacks. Just too many unresolved conflicts. You know girls, in all those so many countries overseas we call autocracies, the leader simply calls the shots and has the police or military around him to enforce his rules. Most people there suffer despite fewer obvious public conflicts. In democracies like here, we argue, and the elected politicians settle their conflicting differences through compromises and voting. The nation as a whole, not too bad. But in our neighborhoods here, the ongoing conflicts were not settled, or settled by fists and guns.

"But wow, there were exceptions. I remember an educator, a long time ago. I remember his name, Marcus Foster. He took a very bad high school here. I think it was Simon Gratz. He developed programs for kids to get jobs. He developed rigorous, advanced classes. He engaged Black teachers. He fought for more school funding. He emphasized learning and personal responsibility. You know? I think I never told that story to Joe, but Marcus was really the beginning of the greatness of our Joe Robinson.

And you know little Miss Arlene, you will be enjoying this just a few short years from now. Joe made a great effort about this, soliciting City Hall for more tax money, the big charitable organizations, the wealthy friends of his billionaire friend. Joe made his case that after sitting and learning all day, at 3p.m. it was **essential** to continue and to expand student access to participation in things that could provide self-confidence, self-esteem, self-pride, joy … that of the extra curricula of sports, art, music, computer technology, shop, and more. Everyone bought in, and it has been a huge Philadelphia success story.

"Well you two. We are all getting sleepy now. Enough. But wait, just one more thing about Joe. In his writings and speaking now, he does at times talk about human nature. He knows kids need a nice combination of love and discipline in their lives. He writes and speaks about teachers needing to convince kids that teachers need to communicate in all sincerity that they really care about them, and that they genuinely want them to learn, sort of like his history teacher, Mr. Washington, had done so effectively with him. And then on the other side to be very firm about maintaining discipline both in and out of the classroom. Joe goes on to talk and write about how people tend, by human nature, to behave in ways that lean towards their personal advantage. That this tendency is expressed in so many different ways. Some, like nurses, feel their personal advantage, their personal fulfillment, is to 'help people'. Others feel that learning a trade well is their way of not just making a living but the joy of self-dignity in doing the work well in itself. All different motivations as each one of us is unique, but underneath it's what motivates us towards our own advantage is how we behave. And at the same time, it's behaving to our own advantage is what is behind so many natural conflicts. Those conflicts are and will be always there but learn to 'resolve them without resorting to violence' is Joe's theme.

"And even with brother William, Joe convinced him through long talks that it would not be to his personal advantage if he were to get shot or go to jail dealing illegal drugs. He also convinced his best friend Charles that it would not be to his eventual advantage if he was caught stealing cars and ending up with jail time and a police record. At the same time, Joe realized that without good job opportunities ahead for them, he had a difficult sell.

Etta suddenly sat up more attentive. "Mama, you said Joe mentioned motivation. He has talked with me recently about how he discovered what makes him tick, about what drives him to do all these wonderful things. He said your teaching and inspiration has always been so important in his finding his own strong motivation to accomplish all these things. So I understand him, but how did he learn how to motivate all those others to get on board? It seems now that we are proud to call ourselves Philadelphians, and Americans, and one out of many, e pluribus unum, our national motto. How Mama?"

"Oh dear. There is so much written about motivation and motivation techniques, but it's usually been applied to employees not what Joe was doing. He told me right before his college graduation that he hit the books on the subject. He reviewed it all with me. I have a good memory still so here goes, ladies.

"He said factors promoting action were getting recognition, using teamwork, a sense of purpose, setting big goals and achieving little ones along the way, social engagement, rewards, being part of something big, incentives, having pride in achievement. That people may like the obtainment of money, of praise, of feeling positive about themselves, of achieving a goal, of feeling good about just making positive efforts towards the achievement goal, of personal power to control the destiny of others, to be socially belonging and accepted by others, by being creative, by avoiding pain or uncomfortable consequences. You see, again we are individually unique, but what Joe had to do with the university leaders, the city politicians, the city-wide top to bottom public school district folks and most importantly the kids was to find what common motivations should work and simply pound away, determined, non-stop. Joe's weekly school presentations somehow turned those kids on. He found the right motivators for each problem. And whenever there might be a glitch, he then determined and told them he would go public with it. He became a pal with successful reporters and TV personalities. He learned the art of successful PR."

Arlene sat still looking befuddled. Etta smiled, then tears came to her eyes.

# 2

Mama Sarah had a difficult time getting up the next morning. Her very long 'chat' with Etta and Arlene was tiring. She felt quite weak in recent days, even with her daily walks, which were getting shorter and shorter. Recently visiting her doctor at Etta's firm demand, she was informed that as is quite normal at her advanced age her heart function was growing weaker. All in all though, she thought her life had not been too bad. Lot of heartache losing her husband so soon, lots of time away from her good job to raise three children, then her daughter and granddaughter and even her great granddaughter all having children without the father at home, her great grandson getting involved with drug gangs. But then there was Joe, always willing to listen to her, accepting her guidance, her teachings about human nature, and now a young celebrity. Not so bad after all, she thought. But tonight, I have to perk up. Joe was now living in a very decent apartment with the love of his life, Theresa, and the two of them were coming over for dinner that evening. Maybe they wanted to discuss wedding plans. She repeated over and over again in her mind: Joe had been the great exception. He accepted the discipline as well as the feeling of love from the grown women in his home. He learned that bad behavior gets punished and good behavior gets rewarded. Yes and no. That simple.

Joe had produced within himself an amazing sense of self-discipline and self -confidence at the young age of fourteen as he developed his basketball talents on the playground courts with the tougher, bigger, older kids – that, along with his daily strength building exercises. He accepted the teachings of his mentor at school, Mr. Robinson, a love of history, where he has been and where it is possible to go. And he was now doing it all, for Philadelphia … and those kids.

Mama Sarah struggled through the rest of the day, felt too weak to take her daily walk, felt she had to lie down a bit before dinner. As she reclined on her couch, softly but out loud her last words were:

"Joe Robinson, I love you."

# Author's Note

I am an American. I think an assimilated American. I was born in South Philadelphia of Italian parents. My father's father died young; his mother never spoke a word of English. Mom and Dad were raised in row homes with no lawn or trees. They both worked hard. They were able to buy a home in the suburbs with a grass lawn front and back. They achieved the American Dream. They saved and were able to send my brother and me to an esteemed private high school and then my brother to Princeton University and me to Duke University and to the University of Pennsylvania's Wharton School.

Commuting everyday a long distance, I remember this about my Mom: she never complained about her role in life; there was no kindergarten then; occasionally, she had to take me to school with her, and I remember in class there were mostly Black kids; I was 4 years old. There was no commotion; they were orderly. For 30 years she taught Puerto Rican and Black kids how to speak and write better English. Mom had beautiful handwriting and spoke perfect English. I am very proud of my mother and father and what they achieved. On their merit.

I would like to think I am still a Philadelphian, but it is hard. Crime, drugs, and guns – stuff we never use to have to think about. I would love to see a renewal. Keep the natural conflicts peaceful. I have a real-life project, sort of like Joe's, but it keeps getting stalled. Nonetheless, if this little novel can do one thing: it's inspiring our Philadelphia leaders to take positive actions to help all those kids now being left behind. They need a good education and job opportunities.

Ben Franklin must be turning over in his grave. "Do something!" his Philadelphia spirit cries.

Printed in the United States
by Baker & Taylor Publisher Services